More shots exploded, Slocum, Monk, and the others dove to the floor as more shots pinged into the cafe.

"So much for bringing the war to them," Slocum said.

"Bastards," Monk bellowed.

"He's dead, Boss," Ratface cried, examining their fallen comrade. "For this we'll make them pay!"

"Who's packin' a gun?" Slocum barked.

"I am," Monk said.

"I got," Dizzy Izzy said.

On all fours, they scrambled over to the shattered windows. Slocum peered out. He saw at least a dozen men shooting at the cafe. They were hidden behind wagons and woodpiles and in rooms in the hotel across the street. Potter had the cafe pinned down pretty damn nicely. . . .

JAKE LOGAN

SLOCUM AND THE
WEST TEXAS PLUNDER

BERKLEY BOOKS, NEW YORK

SLOCUM AND THE WEST TEXAS PLUNDER

A Berkley Book / published by arrangement with
the author

PRINTING HISTORY
Berkley edition / January 1995

ISBN: 0-425-14535-2

BERKLEY®
Berkley Books are published by The Berkley Publishing Group,
200 Madison Avenue, New York, New York 10016.
BERKLEY and the "B" design
are trademarks belonging to Berkley Publishing Corporation.

PRINTED IN THE UNITED STATES OF AMERICA

10 9 8 7 6 5 4 3 2 1

SLOCUM AND THE
WEST TEXAS PLUNDER

1

Slocum's love lay dying.

Her wounds, bullet holes in her chest and belly, would have killed most folks within minutes. Rose Liebowitz, though, was not just anyone. She was a feisty gal of twenty-eight who owned most of the town of Roseville (so named for herself), and was worth a boodle of money.

The bullet holes that riddled her lovely body had been delivered courtesy of Charity "Ma" Fisher and her brood of outlaws, who had shot up the town the day before. The good people of Roseville—led by Rose's sometime lover, John Slocum, had wiped out the Fisher Gang. Slocum had personally blasted Ma Fisher into the great hereafter, and now her ugly head was mounted over the bar in the Roseville Hotel's saloon.

The Fisher Gang was the scourge of the West, a dozen of the lowest, orneriest sidewinders, who made the James brothers and that Bonney kid look like choirboys. The people of Roseville had banded together under Slocum's steady guidance, and stopped them cold, but not before Rose found herself face-to-face with the leader, Ma Fisher, who ventilated her pretty good.

Now she lay in the bed in room six of the hotel she'd financed and built. Financing the place had been easy, since she owned the Roseville Savings and Loan as well, in addition to half the businesses in town, including a profitable whorehouse, three saloons, and twenty thousand acres of prime grazing land. She owned ranches throughout West Texas, a piece of a silver mine in New Mexico, had holdings in shipping companies in Corpus Christi, a stagecoach line in Kansas City, and a slaughterhouse in Fort Worth.

Not bad for a skinny young thing from the slums of New York City's Lower East Side, who'd come west with her father at the age of fifteen to escape the grinding poverty and been forced into prostitution in Little Rock, Arkansas, when he died a year later.

It was in a small Colorado town called Brushwood Gulch that Slocum had first met her. She'd left Arkansas by that time and established in the rowdy town one of the finest and respected whorehouses east of Chicago. It was here that she started building her fortune.

She had too much vision, though, to stay in one place. She saw the limitless possibilities for profit in the state of Texas. Six months later, at the age of twenty-four, she happened upon a tiny wisp of a town called Walnut Springs, little more than a crumbling saloon, general store, and one decrepit church. The closest town of any substance was Stephensville, some two hundred miles away. The territory was in dire need of a town and all it could provide, what with all the ranches there. Within a year, Walnut Springs was gone and Roseville was born in its place.

Across the hall, in another hotel room, Slocum was sharing a bottle with some of Roseville's more influential citizens, including Hiram Quick, who owned half of the Roseville Mercantile (Rose owned the other half) and doubled as the town mayor; Eustace Potter, owner of the Bar-P ranch, one of the biggest and most profitable in the territory, and who was meaner than the harshest Yukon winter; Sam Dumbrille, who managed Rose's bank, a man Slocum wouldn't trust to make the right change from a nickel; Solly Conklin, who managed the three saloons Rose had built; and a thick-waisted, heavily made-up dame of forty-five or so named Esther Howard, who ran the action at the Roseville Happytime Emporium. Although Rose owned the place, she'd hired Esther, who'd been run out of Abilene for reasons nobody knew, to oversee the day-to-day operation. Rose's Happytime Emporium employed six nubile young lasses imported from St. Louis, a skilled Chinese chef, and silks sheets on every bed. The establishment was the town's most profitable business. Esther did a good job—too good; for Rose, before her untimely shooting, had been about to send Esther packing for skimming profits off the top.

Doc Phipps was tending to Rose as the others sat and drank, and demanded that she have no visitors. Slocum rankled at the doc's order. He was more or less in love with the dying woman and wanted to be at her bedside in her hour of need. Yes, he'd run out on her back in Colorado after they'd become an item and started discussing marriage and children and a life on one of her ranches, it was true. He'd only been passing through Roseville when he met up with her again. She'd never truly gotten over him, and when the Fisher Gang descended on Roseville like a plague of ravenous grasshoppers at about the same time, Slocum decided he would stick around to see her and her town through the crisis. He owed her that much. Slocum hadn't planned on her getting shot by Ma Fisher.

"A damn shame, that's what it is," Eustace Potter was growling now. He was a burly, white-haired man of fifty. "Fine woman she is, that Miss Rose."

Potter was the only rancher in the territory who hadn't helped out during the Fisher Massacre, as it was now being called, despite the fact that he had a dozen hands capable with guns. " 'T'aint my headache," he said at the time while other ranchers, Mike Bannon among them, had died defending Roseville. Slocum had little use for Potter.

"Terrible, just terrible," Hiram Quick agreed, patting his damp forehead with a handkerchief. He was short, squat, and had a conspicuous lack of hair, just a few brown strands he vainly combed across his shiny dome.

"Town won't be the same without Miss Rose," Solly Conklin added. He was working on a wad of tobacco and from time to time would spit into a porcelain pitcher usually reserved for wash water. Rose didn't allow chewing or spitting in her hotel rooms, but Slocum said nothing to Conklin.

Sam Dumbrille, who perpetually wore the expression of a cat about to devour a mouse, sipped his whiskey slowly, his beady eyes surveying everyone in the room.

"Always liked her," Dumbrille said in a voice that dripped with insincerity. "Yes indeed."

"The best person I ever worked for," said Esther Howard, applying another inch of makeup to hide yet another wrinkle. Slocum thought she put the stuff on with a cake decorator.

Hypocrites, one and all, Slocum was thinking. Though nobody mentioned it, they all stood to profit from her death. Rose Liebowitz had no blood kin—thus no heirs to her growing empire—that anybody knew of. She'd more than likely made out some sort of last will and testament, they assumed, but wills could be contested if worse came to worst.

Across the hall, Doc Phipps let himself quietly out of Rose's dying room and turned to the assembled group. He was a tall, thin man with a sharp nose and a grave expression. A good sawbones, one of the few in these parts who'd managed to stay off the bottle or his own morphine.

"How is she, Doc?" Eustace Potter asked, though they all knew the answer. Nobody got gut-shot and lived to tell about it.

"Fading fast," Doc Phipps said softly, and looked at Slocum. "She wants to talk to you, John."

Eustace Potter and Esther Howard both stood at the same time Slocum did. Doc Phipps said, "Just Mr. Slocum."

Slocum glared at the others, then followed Doc Phipps into Rose's room, making sure to close the door firmly.

He hung his hat on the doorknob, blocking the key hole just for the hell of it.

In the bed, Rose breathed erratically and with some difficulty. She was paler than an October moon. Slocum went to her and kneeled at her bedside. He took her hand in his. She gave him a gentle squeeze, the best she could do.

"How you feelin', Rose?" Slocum said. Finding words was not easy. He truly felt something mighty for this woman.

Her eyes fluttered open. She swallowed hard, with some pain, and said, "I've been better."

"Doc says you're gonna pull through," Slocum said. "He says—"

"Cut the crap, Slocum," she murmured, a trickle of blood bubbling out the corner of her mouth and sliding down her cheek. Doc Phipps had managed to remove only two of the bullets that had pierced her body. "I'm finished," she said. "Look me in the eye and tell me if I'm not."

Slocum couldn't.

"Look at me anyway, John," Rose said with some effort. Her chest heaved up and down with each labored wheeze for air, sounding like she was trying to breathe underwater.

Slocum looked down into her eyes, watching the flame of life flicker in them.

"You're the only person in the world that I trust," she said, her voice sounding far away. "I got some partners, like Hiram Quick and Eustace Potter, yeah, but dollars to doughnuts they're out there now just waiting for me to kick the bucket."

"True enough, Rosie," Slocum said, fighting back a tear or two.

Across the room, Doc Phipps was washing some of his instruments. Rose said, "Doc, if you don't mind, take a powder."

"But, Miss Rose," he protested. "I have to—"

"You've done your best, Doc, and I'm grateful," Rose said with a cough. "But time is short and I have some things to discuss with Slocum."

Doc Phipps nodded and said, "I understand, Rose." He made himself scarce, making a quick exit into the hall.

Rose squeezed Slocum's hand.

"In my house, behind that lousy portrait of Abe Lincoln in the sitting room, is a safe. Inside is my will. I'm trusting you to see that it gets carried out to the letter, John."

"I'll need the combination first, Rose," Slocum said softly.

"Eighteen left, six right, twenty-one left," she said weakly, the life draining quickly out of her now. "You better write it down."

"I'll remember it," Slocum said dryly.

"Repeat it back to me," she said.

Even close to death, Slocum thought, she could still find a way to put him on the spot. Nonetheless, he repeated it back to her satisfaction.

"I have one living blood relative," she said. "A cousin, back in New York City. The son of my mother's sister. The typhoid took her years back. He was adopted by a couple across the river in Brooklyn, fifteen years ago. Tried to keep tabs on him, but somewhere along the line I lost track. I want you to find him, John, and make sure he lays claim to everything I have. Otherwise, those buzzards out there will grab it for their own. I didn't sweat blood building up my fortune just so those bastards could take it."

"This cousin of yours," Slocum said. "He got a name?"

"Kaminsky," she said. "Samuel David Kaminsky. It's all written in my will, John. Everything you need to know to carry out my last request. It would mean a lot to me."

"I'll do what I can, Rose, you know that," Slocum said.

"There's thirty thousand dollars in the safe, too," she said. "Take it, John, and build a nice life for yourself."

"Ain't never taken a dime from a woman, Rose," Slocum said, not wanting to discuss money even remotely right here and now. "With all due respect."

"Don't be a *schmuck* for two minutes, all right?" she said, mustering her last breaths on his stubborn streak. "Take it, for God's sake. Become a *mensch* for once in your life."

"Sure, Rose," Slocum said. Arguing with Rose, he knew, even as she lay dying, was useless.

"I'm counting on you, Slocum," she said in barely a whisper. "I knew I might eat some lead in this *meshuga* territory, so I made out a will. Don't let those *chazzers,* pigs to you, chisel me out of what's mine."

She gave him a pained smile.

"Watch your back, John," she said, sounding like a body that was fixing to die. "I'm sorry I'll never have your babies, share a life with you. It would have been nice."

With this, she reached out and gave Slocum's testicles a last, healthy squeeze. Then her hand fell away and she died.

Slocum sat there for what seemed like an hour, staring at her arm dangling from the side of the bed. He could call for Doc Phipps, but he knew there was no point. She was gone.

He stood tiredly and placed her arm across her chest. He covered her with the blanket.

"Good-bye, Rose," Slocum whispered, a sob trying to crawl up his throat. He fought it down.

When he stepped out into the hallway, closing the door securely behind him, the others were up and on him like beans on rice.

"Is she dead?" Dumbrille said.

"What's the story, Slocum?" Potter asked at the same time.

"This is just terrible," Hiram Quick said, mopping his brow.

Doc Phipps looked grim. Slocum nodded at him and started walking down the hallway to the stairs. The others followed him like hungry piglets, rapid-firing questions at him.

"What happens now?"

"The bank's business can't wait," said Sam Dumbrille.

"How do I keep the saloons going?" Solly Conklin wanted to know.

"And the cathouse," Esther Howard added.

Slocum turned to them, trying to bottle up the anger that could rip them all into tiny pieces. He jammed his hat onto his head.

"She's dead," Slocum said grimly. "But I wouldn't start celebrating just yet."

Eustace Potter's eyes squinted into evil slits.

"Meanin' what?" he said.

"Meanin' I know what's on your narrow little minds," he said. "But before you start countin' the money, you should know Rose Liebowitz has blood kin livin' in New York City, and I'm aimin' to see he gets what's rightfully his."

"Did she leave a will?" Hiram Quick asked.

"She did," Slocum said.

"Then let's take a look-see," Eustace Potter piped up. "Couldn't hurt."

Slocum walked up to Potter, who stood a solid three inches taller, and poked a finger in his chest.

"It might, Potter," Slocum said. "Far's I'm concerned."

Potter's left hand dropped to his holster, where a shiny new Colt sat waiting for action. Slocum knew from experience that Potter was too gutless to make a move. Instead, Potter paid his band of lowlifes to do his killing.

"Do it, Potter," Slocum said, egging him on. "Give me a good excuse."

Potter's hand dropped benignly to his side. He'd be no more trouble. For now.

"As the law in this town of Roseville," Slocum said, "and seeing how long it would take a federal judge to get here, I'm going to take a look at her will and act on it accordingly."

"And when did you become the law in this town?" Potter asked indignantly.

"Right before your marshal, Chester Perkey, died fighting the Fisher Gang," Slocum said. "He deputized me."

No one chose to argue the matter. Slocum preferred it that way. He said to Doc Phipps, "Doc, take care of the burial arrangements. Jewish people like to be buried quickly, so I've heard."

"Rose and I discussed it," Doc Phipps said, genuine sadness in his tone. "I'll handle it."

"Thanks," Slocum said. He turned and walked down the stairs to the lobby, then made his way outside and headed for the house Rose had built for herself down at the edge of town.

Potter, Hiram Quick, Miss Esther Howard, and the rest came downstairs after Slocum. They lingered in the doorway of the hotel but didn't follow him.

"Something about that man I don't like," Sam Dumbrille said.

"You and me both," Eustace Potter said. "We may have to do somethin' about it."

"Oh dear, this is terrible," Hiram Quick said nervously, wiping sweat from his ruddy face. "After all this tragedy, how could you even think—"

"Shut up, Hiram," Esther Howard said.

Rose was right—the portrait of Lincoln was pretty lousy, as though either the artist or Lincoln had been drunk at the time. But just as Rose had promised, behind it was a safe.

Slocum spun the dial, using the combination Rose had given him, and opened it. Inside were some deeds, a bundle of cash, some miscellaneous papers with fancy business letterheads, and finally, Rose's last will and testament.

Slocum poured himself a brandy from a crystal bottle Rose kept handy, then sat and read over the will. He was astonished to learn that Rose had had the foresight to name one John Slocum as temporary executor of her estate, until such a time as her only heir could be located.

And what an estate it was. Slocum was amazed to discover the true extent of her holdings. The woman was worth much more than the million dollars she'd said she was worth.

Intermingled among the property deeds and papers was a faded photograph of what could only have been Rose her own self at the age of ten or thereabouts. She was sitting on the stoop of a grimy, crumbling tenement. There was a mischievous smirk on her face, which was somewhat gaunt. Still, Slocum could see the seeds of beauty that would flourish in the years to come. He fought back the tears again.

He finished his brandy and shoved all of Rose's papers into his pocket, as well as the bundle of cash, and made his way outside. Somehow, he didn't feel secure about leaving the goods in the safe, what with certain parties in town being less than honest. He'd already decided he didn't want to stay in Rose's house—too many memories there. His room at the hotel would do him all right. Later, after sundown and with a bottle or two in the privacy of his room, he would treat himself to some serious grieving.

Now, though, there were things to be done.

Slocum walked down Main Street to the telegraph office. Inside, Mortimer Bagley was tapping out a message. Bagley was an officious little fellow from Georgia, a fussy fat man born to be a thorn in the side of his fellow human beings. A pretty young woman, with blond hair piled high, was standing behind the counter, wringing a silk handkerchief anxiously between her fingers. Slocum knew her. She was Melody Daniels, the widow of a rancher who'd been bit by a rattlesnake one day while working the range, miles from home.

With a small child, there was no way Miss Melody could run the place. She'd sold out to Eustace Potter (swindled, Rose always claimed but never elaborated), and Rose gave her a job running the dress shop. She and her three-year-old daughter lived in a small frame house at the other end of Main Street.

"Will that get there today?" Miss Melody asked Bagley anxiously. "It's very important that my sister in San Angelo knows we're coming on the next available train."

"It's already there," Mortimer said. He was a cranky old cuss. "What time they get it to yer sister ain't no problem of mine."

Slocum tapped Miss Melody lightly on the arm. He took off his hat and said, "Excuse me, Miss Melody, but did I overhear you say you were fixin' to leave town?"

"I'm afraid so, Mr. Slocum," she responded.

"But why?" he asked. "Don't mean to be familiar, and I know we ain't well acquainted, but I always got the impression you liked it here."

"Oh, I do," she said. "Very much. It's just that with poor Miss Rose gone—what a wonderful woman she was, God rest her precious soul—well, my job at the dress shop appears to be in question."

"There's no question, Miss Melody," Slocum said. "The dress shop is yours now—lock, stock, and hemlines."

"Mine?" she asked, looking perplexed.

"Rose would've wanted you to have it," Slocum said. "I'm sure of that."

"That's very sweet of you to offer, Mr. Slocum," Miss Melody said, "but have you the authority to do this?"

"No, not really," Slocum said, "but there's nobody who'll tell me I can't. Also, Miss Rose made me the temporary executor of her estate until we can locate her kin. When we do, I'm sure he'll agree to my decision."

"Mr. Slocum," she said, smiling nervously, not quite believing her good fortune. "I don't know what to say."

"You can start by canceling that message to your sister."

"Yes, of course," she said, and turned to Mortimer Bagley. "Mr. Bagley—"

"I heared, I heared," Bagley said irritably. "Got to charge you for it all the same, though."

"This one's on me," Slocum piped up.

"I don't know how to thank you, Mr. Slocum," she said, blushing. "Could you perhaps come to dinner this evening?"

"Thank you just the same, ma'am," Slocum said, "but I think I'd rather be sort of alone with my thoughts tonight." He left out the part with the bottle or two. "Some other time, if it ain't inconvenient."

"Of course," she said, sounding embarrassed. "How could I be so insensitive. Miss Rose and yourself were . . . well, I . . . I understand, Mr. Slocum."

She reached up and kissed him on the cheek, and gave his hand a squeeze. "You're a good man, Mr. Slocum. Please accept my deepest condolences."

She turned to go. Slocum instinctively watched her as she left, closing the door behind herself and flashing him a small smile. The bell over the door tinkled, and she was gone.

"Nice girl," Mortimer commented. "Was I you, I wouldn't mourn too long."

"Was I *you*," Slocum said, picking up a pencil and a blank piece of paper, "I'd mind my own business." He started writing.

"No law against speakin' my mind," Bagley sniffed. "Be a dollar-fifty for her message."

"Got to send one of my own," Slocum said. He wrote a few lines, signed his name, and handed it to Bagley.

Bagley peered through the top half of his bifocals. " 'To: Alphonse Bupp, Pinkerton Detective Agency, Kansas City,' " Bagley half-read, half-muttered. He studied the rest of the message, counting out every letter.

"Be four dollars and twenty cents," Bagley said. "With Miss Melody's charges, five dollars and seventy cents."

Slocum reached into his pocket, removed some bills and change, and paid Bagley. He didn't really have to—Rose owned half the telegraph office as well.

Bagley sat and started tapping out the message. Slocum waited patiently. He'd requested an immediate response from Alphonse Bupp, an old acquaintance from the war who'd joined up with the Pinkertons some years back. If anyone could find Rose's cousin, Samuel David Kaminsky, in the depths of New York, it was the Pinkertons.

Later, after Slocum had left, Eustace Potter paid the telegraph office a visit with a couple of ranch hands, mean bastards who drank a lot and neither smiled nor shaved.

"Miss Rose has some blood kin," Bagley told them, averting the hostile glances of Potter's men. "A cousin in some place called Brooklyn, New York. Slocum has the Pinkertons tryin' to locate him."

"Think they will?" Potter asked.

"Damned if I know," Bagley said.

"Slocum still bunkin' in at the hotel?" Potter cleaned his dirty fingernails with the tip of the ink pen.

"Ain't heard otherwise," Bagley said.

Potter turned and walked out, his men following dutifully a few steps behind.

Stacks Jensen had joined on with Eustace Potter's Bar-P six months ago. He was a nasty, thieving, murdering, raping son of a booger who'd slit open his own mother's belly to warm his hands. Potter liked him immediately. Ostensibly a ranch hand, Jensen was hired mostly to kill sodbusters and rustlers and anyone else who got in Potter's way. In the half a year since he started working for Potter, Jensen had planted four people, including one sheep farmer's young daughter who'd seen his face as he gunned down her father. Potter didn't like witnesses. Stacks got a two-dollar bonus.

It was a little after midnight as Stacks Jensen crept down the hallway toward Slocum's room. He'd made the desk clerk unconscious a minute earlier with the butt of his Colt .45.

Jensen knew that Slocum had retired to his room a few hours before with two bottles of whiskey, no doubt to mourn the passing of his girlfriend, Miss Rose. Jensen could almost understand; that woman had been some sweet piece of merchandise. He'd never raped anyone nearly as pretty as her.

By this time, Jensen reasoned, Slocum would be passed out cold. This one would be easier than plucking a chicken.

That Slocum was in room 10 on the second floor was no secret. He'd been holing up there since coming to town.

Jensen approached the door. The locks on it were kid stuff to a powerful man like Stacks Jensen. He kicked the door in easily with his left boot, and took one wide step inside. He could see the outline of the bed in the darkness, and Slocum huddled under the covers. He squeezed off four shots into the blanketed form and was momentarily puzzled to see a blizzard of feathers spew into the air. He threw back the blanket and saw two mortally wounded pillows.

"Looking for somebody?" a voice said behind him.

Before Jensen could completely turn and fire again, Slocum opened up with both barrels of his rifle, hitting the bastard square in the chest. A huge roar filled the small room as Jensen flew backward onto the bed, dead before he even hit the goose-down mattress.

Slocum checked to see if Jensen was still breathing. Outside, dogs began to bark, and lamplight flared up in windows. Jensen was finished.

The desk clerk, a thin, goggle-eyed youth of nineteen named Harvey Teller, peered nervously into the room, holding a bloody handkerchief to his head.

"Are you all right, Mr. Slocum?" Harvey asked.

Slocum nodded and lit the lamp, gave the dead man on the bed a closer look.

"Who is he?" Harvey asked.

"One of Potter's boys," Slocum said. "Johnson, Jensen, something like that. Seen him around. I was afraid this might happen."

"Should I get Doc Phipps?"

"Won't be necessary," Slocum said. "I'll be needing a new room, though."

Harvey swallowed hard, loosening his collar. "I'll get you a key."

"Damn shame," Slocum said. "Damn shame."

"What's that, Mr. Slocum?" Harvey asked.

"Miss Rose ain't even cold yet, and we're already fightin' over her money," Slocum said sadly.

2

"No, no, no *no,* Samuel!" Professor Stossel cried, waving the bow of his violin angrily. "If you're ever to learn how to play ze violin, my son, zen you must learn discipline." Professor Stossel's German accent was thicker than a slab of Wiener schnitzel. The professor proceeded to play a melody by Mozart. "Slide the bow over the strings gracefully. Remember, Samuel, you are not chopping down from a tree. A violin is like a woman. Stroke it softly for ze best results."

Samuel David Kaminsky sighed and tried his best to play his violin along with the good professor, who had been giving him lessons for nearly twelve years, from the time Sammy was eight.

Sammy was a thin, sallow-faced lad who had never ventured beyond the teeming streets of Williamsburg, Brooklyn, approximately thirty or so square city blocks, though there had been a trolley trip to Coney Island the summer before. He weighed 130 pounds soaking wet and stood nearly six feet tall. Unruly black hair fell over his huge brown eyes, which peered out from behind thick wire-rimmed spectacles. Even with them, he squinted.

Sammy sighed and started to accompany Professor Stossel. This Mozart piece was especially difficult. Sammy did okay until the third measure, then missed a couple of notes.

"Twelve years," Stossel snorted angrily, "and you shtill have learned nothink! Daydreaming, all ze time daydreaming."

Professor Stossel held his violin and bow in one hand and clunked Sammy squarely on the head with the other. Sammy shook his head and played the rest of the piece perfectly. Professor Stossel was good for at least six head clunkings in the course of a one-hour lesson. Today was a good day—there had only been four. Sammy took this as a sign of progress.

Professor Stossel put his violin down on the kitchen table and pulled a pocket watch from his vest. "Three o'clock," he said. "Zat is all for today, Samuel." He started packing up his violin. "I vant you should practice for another hour after I leave."

"Yes, Professor," Sammy replied, though he had no intention of doing anything of the kind. Uncle Jake and Aunt Meema needed him at the restaurant. He reached into the pocket of his pants and fished out fifty cents, which Aunt Meema had given him to pay the professor, as he did every week.

Professor Stossel took the money and dropped it into a little change purse. Sammy helped the old man on with his coat.

"You have so much talent, Samuel," Professor Stossel said as he put on his big black fedora. Summer or winter, the little old German always dressed the same. "If only you vould spend more time playing instead of daydreaming, you could be playing every opera house on Fourteenth Street. You play vell enough, I zuppose, if playing in a beer garten is your goal in zis life."

"Oh, I don't think Aunt Meema would let me play in a beer garden," Sammy said in all seriousness. "I do play in the restaurant, though."

"I am vell avare that you perform for pennies and nickels," Professor Stossel snorted. "Soon you vill end up in the honky-tonkeys on ze Bowery and then on street corners."

Sammy shrugged. "The customers seem to like my music," he said.

"Piffle," Stossel said, and opened the apartment door to leave. "I vill see you in a veek, and next time try and stay avake. Think big, my young dumbhead. Zere iz a vorld outside this Brooklyn, New York. Zat's why you daydream, Samuel. You yearn for more out of life than serving borscht and blintzes to people. Keep in mind, my little *swinehunt:* Zat violin you are holding can take you to all ze places you dream about."

With that, the exact same parting shot that Professor Stossel had delivered each and every week for twelve years, the doddering old maestro departed. Sammy waited for his footsteps to fade away as Stossel went down the four flights of noisy tenement stairs. Sammy rushed to the living room window of the cramped apartment and watched Professor Stossel leave the building and cross Knickerbocker Avenue to the trolley back to Manhattan Island. The truth be told, Sammy never dreamed about lands outside Brooklyn. He was perfectly content on the crowded, noisy streets of Williamsburg. Wide open spaces, like that day at Coney Island, made him sweat anxiously.

Once Professor Stossel was out of sight, Sammy packed up his violin and grabbed his cap. Jamming the cap on his head, he went out the door, the violin tucked safely under one arm, and made his way down onto the bustling street. Knickerbocker Avenue was alive with street merchants peddling their wares, everything from fresh fish and vegetables to three-piece suits and dresses, all off the backs of wagons and from pushcarts.

Clutching his violin, Sammy slithered his way through the throngs of shoppers like a snake through a rock pile. He loved the sights and smells of Knickerbocker Avenue. He passed Abe the pickle merchant.

"Buy a kosher pickle," Abe chanted. "Dill pickles, garlic pickles, sour pickles, gherkins, sweet and sweeter."

Sammy purchased for a penny a nice fat dill Abe plucked from the barrel especially for him. Sammy munched happily, juice squirting in every direction.

"Nothing gives both so much pleasure and so much heartburn as a nice pickle," Abe exclaimed. "Happy ulcer, brother."

Sammy finished his pickle and turned left on Herkimer Street. The steps of the tenements were lined with dozens of young toughs spoiling for trouble and ready to pummel anyone weaker who might be carrying a few pennies. A skinny young guy like Sammy carrying a violin presented an attractive target.

Nonetheless, Sammy proceeded unmolested down Herkimer Street until a burly Irish lad of about sixteen, his nose already as red as his hair, appeared directly in front of him, brandishing a knife. Sammy had never seen him before; few Irishmen ventured onto Herkimer Street, a predominantly Jewish enclave.

"Give me all yer money, boyo," the thug demanded, "or I'll cut yer from neck to nuts."

Before Sammy could even react, two shadows fell upon the young punk. Ratface Cohen and Dizzy Izzy Farkus grabbed the Irisher from behind, one around the neck and the other around the waist. Ratface Cohen, a scrapper of nineteen, brought his knee up and smashed it into the small of the the guy's back, while Dizzy Izzy snapped the Irisher's arm and sent his knife skittering across the sidewalk. Together they dragged him into the alley and pounded him into jelly, kicking and beating him into a bloody Irish stew. Ratface tore a chunk of wood off a broken wagon wheel and started beating the intruder over the head with it.

Sammy watched the sick spectacle without comment. This was the violent playlet he'd seen acted out dozens of time on the hazardous Brooklyn streets.

"You touch this guy again," Ratface warned the inert form moaning in the alley, pointing to Sammy, "and I'll kick you till yer dead."

Ratface Cohen, leaving his friend Dizzy Izzy to deliver the last few blows to Sammy's attacker, wiped his bloody hands on his knickers and said to Sammy, "Monk wants ta see you."

Dizzy Izzy, as tough as they come, grabbed the semi-conscious Irisher by the collar and lifted him groggily to his feet. The Irisher stood erect just long enough for Dizzy Izzy to slip on a set of brass knuckles.

"A little going-away present," Dizzy Izzy said, and delivered a ferocious blow to the Irisher's belly, followed by another to his jaw. Dizzy Izzy automatically stepped back as the thug's breakfast came up and spewed out of his mouth. He sagged to the ground in a bloody, vomit-covered heap. Passersby ignored the grisly scene, knowing better than to intrude.

Dizzy Izzy came up on Sammy's left, with Ratface Cohen at his right. Together they escorted him wordlessly down the street to a boarded-up storefront with the words "Monks Pet Stor" crudely lettered over the door.

Ratface Cohen knocked twice, then paused for a few seconds and knocked three more times. The door to the storefront opened as if by magic. Ratface and Dizzy Izzy ushered Sammy inside. The door just as mysteriously slammed shut behind them, and they were engulfed in near darkness. In the back of the empty store a lone candle burned on top of a battered desk, throwing ghostly light onto the face of a man sitting behind it, smoke puffing from his cigarette. It was a sinister face, with a jagged scar cutting from below the left eye all the way down to the corner of the man's mouth. Most of the man's right ear was missing, leaving a mishappen, fleshy stub. A battered derby sat cockily on top of his head.

Dozens and dozens of skinny cats roamed around the place, fighting and mating and chasing rats. One sat purring on the man's lap. The scarred man stroked it tenderly.

"Here he is, Monk," Dizzy Izzy said, releasing Sammy's arm. "Just like you wanted."

"Fine," the man said. "Now yous can go."

Ratface Cohen and Dizzy Izzy made hasty exits, leaving Sammy alone with this horror of a man.

"How are you, Sammy?" the man said. "How are the lessons going?"

"Me, I can't complain," Sammy replied, used to the sight of this scary-looking man. "Professor Stossel, he's another story."

A dry chuckle rasped from the man's throat. Sammy squatted on the floor and opened his violin case. He took the instrument out and grabbed the bow. A black cat hopped onto his shoulder; another rubbed against his leg. Sammy stroked the one on his shoulder a few times and then gently plucked it away and deposited it on the floor. Monk loved his cats. The cat scurried away as Sammy tuned his violin.

"Play the one I like so much," the man said. "You know."

Indeed Sammy did. He was playing for his best audience, the terror of Williamsburg—Monk Westman. Monk was the thirty-year-old son of a rabbi who held the neighborhood in a grip of fear with his violent gang of street thugs. He extorted money from every merchant, pushcart peddler, and shop owner operating in his self-proclaimed kingdom. He controlled the gambling, the prostitution, and every other vice in the neighborhood, reaping enormous profits. The pet store was a front. Monk Westman, whose real name was Moses Bernard Schwartz, boasted an army of some hundred men, neighborhood guys who pillaged Williamsburg like drunken Cossacks on orders from Monk. Every business in a radius of fifty blocks paid Monk Westman tribute of one kind or another—cold cash or baskets of food or whatever goods they could offer. Failure to pay usually meant a cracked skull or a broken leg. Those foolhardy enough to resist or complain to the police usually ended up floating facedown in the East River. Indeed, Monk had most of the police on his payroll, and those that weren't never squawked about the ones who were.

"Play it, Sam," Monk Westman said in almost a whisper. The Monk, Sammy knew, had two great loves—cats and music. It was his love for the latter that helped keep Sammy in one piece. Nobody dared lay a hand on what Monk Westman felt was his personal property.

Sammy started to play a song called "Waltz Me Again, Tillie," a slow, soulful melody that was popular in the music halls of Manhattan. As Sammy played, more cats jumped onto Monk's lap and fought for space. Monk, as the melody continued, began to weep shamelessly, crying his eyes out. Sammy always felt that Monk was mourning something or somebody. His was not an easy life.

Sammy finished "Waltz Me Again, Tillie" and started playing another slow, sad melody from the old country in Russia, one that Aunt Meema used to sing to him. Monk started crying even harder, his hot teardrops plopping onto his cats. Each string Sammy plucked on his violin also plucked a string in Monk's normally cold heart.

The only pets in Monk's pet store office were his dozens of felines, and none of them were for sale. Not that Monk ever got any offers; both the residents of the neighborhood and the police knew that Monk used the joint as his base of operations. Now Sammy stroked his violin and made sweet music, and the murderous gang leader hugged his cats and cried like a baby.

In the middle of the tune, the door flew open and two of Monk's boys, Aaron Klepper and Gaspipe Rudnick, so named for his habit of tearing off sections of the same to use on late or reluctant payers, burst into the place.

Klepper, one of Monk's meaner little toadies, blurted out, "Hey, Monk—Old Man Schindler's holdin' out on us again, second week in a row, the old bastard. Me an' Gaspipe—"

Sammy stopped playing. He saw Monk stiffen angrily. Sammy could almost feel Monk's rage bubbling up to the surface. So, too, could his cats. They leapt off his lap and skittered away to hide under the nearest piece of old furniture.

Monk said serenely, "Didn't I say nobody comes in when the kid is fiddlin'?"

"Yeah, sure, Monk," Klepper said breathlessly. "But Old Man Schindler—"

Monk stood slowly, and even in the darkness of the room, Sammy could see the hateful stare he directed at Aaron Klepper.

"Don't you remember me sayin' no one, but *no* one comes in here when the kid's playin', no matter what?" Monk rasped.

"Guess I forgot, Monk," Klepper stammered. "I just thought—"

"I do the thinkin' around here," Monk barked, and all three of them—Gaspipe, Klepper, and Sammy—flinched. Monk pulled a derringer from the pocket of his baggy pants and squeezed off a shot. The bullet smashed into Aaron Klepper's kneecap, sending bone chips and blood flying. Klepper crashed to the floor, howling in pain and clutching his wounded knee. Gaspipe Rudnick needed no further convincing. He made a hasty—and wise—exit. Klepper continued to wail. Sammy felt the blood drain from his face and an overpowering need to vomit.

Monk growled, "Now from this day on, every time you take a step, you'll remember what I said." He turned to Sammy. His voice smooth as velvet he said, "Go ahead, Samuel."

Sammy stared in shock at Aaron Klepper, writhing in agony on the sawdust- and cat-shit-covered floor, barely hearing Monk's words.

"I said start playin'," Monk repeated patiently, though there was a dangerous edge in his voice.

In a fog, Sammy started scraping the bow against the violin strings, and the notes that resulted didn't even remotely sound like a melody. Monk didn't seem to care. He sat down again, pocketing the derringer. Slowly, his cats started returning. Aaron Klepper crawled, painfully, toward the door, groaning all the way.

Monk said to him, "Don't get no blood on my cats, Klepper."

Klepper inched his way agonizingly to the door, then managed to stand on his one good leg to twist the doorknob.

"You or Gaspipe tell anyone you saw me blubbering, I'll kill you both," Monk said to Klepper.

Klepper whimpered and fell to the floor. He crawled out the door and kicked it shut behind him. Sammy played, sounding like a chicken being butchered. The pickle churned sourly in his stomach.

"You sound a little off today, Samuel," Monk commented, petting one of his cats.

"Must be something I ate," Sammy said, his hands shaking too much to produce anything listenable on his violin.

"Must be," Monk agreed.

3

Sammy had got barely ten feet down Herkimer Street before he grabbed the lid off a garbage can and spewed the contents of his stomach, which included a breakfast of herring and eggs and a lunch of one huge pickle.

He'd never seen anyone shot before. The sight of blood, even that from a chicken, made him queasy. It shouldn't have. Violence was an everyday sight on the congested, angry streets of Brooklyn. Guns, though, bothered Sammy. Such a black object could do so much damage. Sammy vowed never to go near one.

The truth was the violence in general had a bad effect on him, unlike most of the boys who inhabited the teeming tenements of Williamsburg, who thrived on it. Thank God Aunt Meema didn't know about his command performances for Monk Westman. Sammy knew she'd never understand the price he paid for not being devoured by the violent streets and spat out like so much gristle on a side of pastrami.

Fogelman the fish peddler, a short, squat man, bald except for a few sparse strands of hair hanging over his forehead, happened by, dragging his pushcart down the street.

"Fresh fi-i-i-i-sh!" he sang in a tired, lilting voice.

"Tuna fish! Catfish! Swordfish if you wish! Pikefish, troutfish, and if flounder is your dish, come see me."

An old lady with a face like a bucket of spit threw open her tenement window and screeched, "Gimme a codfish."

Fogelman opened a small wooden hatch on the pushcart and pulled out a fish so rotten Sammy could smell it ten feet away. He started retching anew.

Fogelman wrapped the fish tightly in some white wax paper and tossed it up to the lady hanging out the window. She caught it with ease, then tossed some pennies down to him.

The fishmonger caught most of them and scrambled on the sidewalk for the rest. He retrieved them, and saw Sammy clutching his stomach with one arm and wiping his mouth on the sleeve of the other.

"You do not look so good, my friend," Fogelman said, shoving the pennies into his pocket.

"To tell the truth, I've felt better," Sammy mumbled, his stomach heaving. The aroma of rotten fish from Fogelman's pushcart didn't help any.

In the two years he'd been fiddling for Monk Westman, Sammy, while well aware of Monk's feared reputation in the neighborhood, had always been shielded from the violence Monk was famous for. It was probably just a matter of time, Sammy knew, before he was swept up in one of Monk's bloody tidal waves. The man was just plain unpredictable and was capable of anything. Who could tell, the day might come when Monk would put a bullet in Sammy's kneecap. One sour note could cost dearly.

"I got just what you need," Fogelman said, rummaging through his pushcart bin. He pulled out a smelly little fish. "A nice herring will fix you up. The herring swims in calm waters, so it's good for your nerves. A bluefish, that you don't want."

The stench from the herring, which had seen better days, provoked a fresh round of puking.

"No, thank you," Sammy groaned weakly.

"Suit yourself," Fogelman said with a shrug. He tossed the herring back into the bin and dragged his pushcart away. "Fre-e-e-e-ssh fi-i-i-sssh!" he chanted, his voice fading as he peddled his way down the cobblestone streets.

Sammy sat rocking on the curb for a minute or two before he felt well enough to continue.

"I don't think this neighborhood agrees with me," Sammy murmured to no one in particular.

Inside Levinsky's Dairy Restaurant, bearded Jewish men, local merchants and businessmen, munched on *blintzes*, *challah*, smoked salmon, and cream cheese. They slurped beet-red *borscht* and pea soup so thick that a spoon could stand in it. They talked politics and argued Jewish law, eating, belching, and gesturing a great deal with their hands.

The place was a beehive of activity. Sammy closed the door and tried to steer clear of the harried waiters, carrying trays of steaming food and weaving around one another like greased worms. Other waiters swept dirty dishes onto trays at recently vacated tables. Sammy's Uncle Jake Levinsky sat behind the cash register, peering over half spectacles at a customer's check. Uncle Jake was in his late forties, just going to fat, the greasy apron he wore barely concealing his gut.

"One *kasha varnishka,* one potato leek soup, one glass tea," he said, tallying the bill in his head. "Thirty cents."

The customer, a man dressed in a business suit, opened his coat. Sammy saw the shiny police badge gleam in the afternoon sun.

"Make it nothing," Uncle Jake said. "For members of New York's finest, it's on the house."

The policeman nodded and left. Sammy walked over to the counter, where Uncle Jake was stealing change from the register. Sammy opened his violin case and pulled out his violin. Among other chores he did at his aunt and uncle's restaurant, Sammy was called upon to

play his violin for the gratification of the customers. Of
course, Uncle Jake added a few cents to their bills for it.
Entertainment charge, he called it.

"Humph," Uncle Jake snorted. "Only in America can a
man wear a piece of tin and eat for nothing." He turned to
his nephew. "Very nice of you to drop by," he said with
a touch of acid. "Your lesson ended an hour ago. If it's
not too much trouble, maybe you'd like to tell me where
you've been?"

"Here and there," Sammy said meekly.

"Here and there he says," Uncle Jake snorted. "*Oy*,
such a little *schlemiel* you are. Never mind the violin,
Mr. Here and There. Go help your aunt in the kitch-
en."

"Yes, Uncle Jake," Sammy said, putting his violin away
and stashing it behind the counter. He made his way
to the kitchen in back, dodging Max the waiter, who
swerved and almost dropped three orders of *blintzes* and
sour cream.

"You should watch where I'm going," Max the waiter
snapped. "What's the matter for you?"

"Sorry, Max," Sammy said. In the kitchen, Aunt Meema
was screaming at the cook, a short, dark little Albanian
named Lazlo, who scowled a lot and sweated into the food.
Sammy, for that reason, rarely ate at Levinsky's Dairy
Restaurant. In a corner, old ladies sat and peeled onions
and potatoes. Another sat at a table making *blintzes*—
pot cheese wrapped in a flour crust, to be fried later to
a golden brown.

Aunt Meema, short and squat with a round face and her
hair piled into a severe bun, finished yelling at Lazlo, then
turned her attention to the old lady making the *blintzes*.

"*Oy*, you're making those *blintzes* too big, Esther," she
complained. "Try to remember we're feeding Jews here,
not elephants."

The kitchen door to the alley opened and in came
Noodleman, the bread maven, carrying half a dozen boxes
filled with rye, pumpernickel, and other baked delights.

"Where do you want these, Mrs. Levinsky?" Noodleman said, setting them down on the counter as he did every afternoon.

"Right there is fine," Aunt Meema said.

Noodleman pulled an invoice from the pocket of his coat and said to Aunt Meema, "That's twenty dollars and forty cents you owe me, Mrs. Levinsky."

Aunt Meema started stirring a huge, boiling pot of pea soup and said, "You should kindly put it on my account, Mr. Noodleman."

"This I can't do, Mrs. Levinsky," Noodleman said. "You owe me for three days already."

"So what's three days for old friends?" Aunt Meema said with a shrug of her wide shoulders. "I knew you when you were just a little *pisher* in short pants, Lester Noodleman. This is how you treat an old friend of your mother's? Let me ask you, Lester. Who gave you a silver dollar for your *bar mitzvah*?"

"You did, Mrs. Levinsky," Noodleman said.

"And who continued to do business with you after you took over the bakery when your father, he should rest in peace, passed away?"

"You did, Mrs. Levinsky," Noodleman said with a tired sigh.

"And who told Zuckerman the baker on Linden Avenue no when he offered me the same bread for two cents less a loaf?"

"You did, Mrs. Levinsky."

"So this is the thanks I get?" Aunt Meema said, on the verge of tears. She started wiping her eyes with her dirty apron. "I changed your diapers when you were no bigger than one of these *blintzes*." She picked one up and held it in Noodleman's face, more tears streaking her plump cheeks.

This was the point, Sammy knew from experience, where Noodleman usually caved in. Not that Aunt Meema wouldn't pay Noodleman at some point—she always did, eventually, and would have this very day had Greenberg the cheese maven not demanded his own payment of sixty dollars earlier that morning. Someone always had to wait, but all were paid sooner or later. Aunt Meema was good at keeping her suppliers at bay long enough to keep the restaurant going for at least another day.

"All right already, enough with the tears, Mrs. Levinsky," Noodleman said, disgusted at his own weakness. "You can pay me tomorrow, but tomorrow for sure." He took off his hat, wiped his brow in the steaming kitchen, and slapped the hat back onto his head. As he was going out the door, he added, "And if not, then Zuckerman can *have* your business, and with pleasure."

Noodleman stormed out, knowing Mrs. Levinsky had bested him once again.

"Why do you torture him so, Aunt Meema?" Sammy said, donning an apron. He started scrubbing some pots in the sink.

"Someday, when you have to earn your own living, you'll understand," Aunt Meema said with a cluck of her tongue. She continued stirring the pea soup. "I'm sure your Uncle Jake already asked you why you're so late, so I won't."

"Thank you," Sammy said, rubbing grease off a steel pot in a huge sink full of hot water.

"And just what do you think you're doing?" Aunt Meema asked.

Sammy studied the soapy pot quizzically. "I think I'm cleaning this pot."

"Then here's another question," Aunt Meema snapped. "*Why* are you washing that pot?"

"Uncle Jake said—"

"And who told you to listen to your Uncle Jake?" she wanted to know. "What do you think, Samuel, that I pay that Professor Stossel fifty cents a lesson so you can ruin your hands washing pots? Take off that apron and start with the violin."

Dropping the pot into the water, Sammy said, "All right, so I'll start with the violin."

• • •

Ten minutes later, Sammy stood and played one melody after another, mostly Beethoven and Mozart Professor Stossel had taught him. At one point he tried to break into a popular favorite called "Be My Lovey-Dovey," until Uncle Jake angrily snapped at him in Yiddish.

"How many times have I got to tell you, Sammy? You play fast, the customer eats fast. He eats fast, he gets indigestion. He gets indigestion, he doesn't come back. He doesn't come back, we go out of business."

Sammy went back to playing the classics.

Sammy was swinging when a tall, serious-looking man came into the restaurant. The man seemed naturally to command respect. Not a cop of any kind, Sammy knew instinctively, but a man of authority all the same. The man said something to Uncle Jake, who immediately looked shocked.

Uncle Jake grabbed Max the waiter by the arm and whispered something into his ear. Sammy couldn't hear it over the din of the loud customers and his own violin playing. Max the waiter made a beeline into the kitchen. A few seconds later, Aunt Meema came out and went hurriedly to Uncle Jake. She said something to the tall man, then Uncle Jake said something, then Aunt Meema snapped at Uncle Jake.

All three talked for a few minutes. Then Aunt Meema came over and gently took Sammy's arm, stopping him in the middle of a C-minor.

Aunt Meema said gravely, "Come, Samuel, some talking we need to do."

Uncle Jake put Max the waiter in charge, reluctantly, and led the tall stranger to one of the back back tables, near the kitchen. He sat. Sammy sat.

"What is this all about, Aunt Meema?" Sammy asked, looking nervous. He was convinced that this man had come to inquire about Aaron Klepper's recent accident.

Aunt Meema said, "This man wants to ask you some

questions, Samuel. I want you should answer him honestly and politely."

Sammy wasn't going to answer him at all. He knew the price he'd pay if he squealed on Monk Westman, if indeed that's what this man wanted him to do.

"Is your name Samuel David Kaminsky?" the man asked.

Sammy knew better than to deny this. "Yes," he said.

"Does the name Rose Liebowitz mean anything to you?"

Sammy looked at Aunt Meema searchingly. What did any Rose Liebowitz have to do with Monk Westman?

"No, I don't think so," Sammy said to the policeman.

"According to my sources, Rose Liebowitz was your first cousin," the man said. "If you *are* Samuel David Kaminsky, that is."

"Oh, I am, I am," Sammy said. He turned to Aunt Meema. "I am, aren't I?"

Aunt Meema said to the tall man, "Maybe I should explain it to him." She grabbed a chair and sat. Uncle Jake stood nearby, saying nothing.

"You know, Samuel, how I've told you that you're not really our son, that we took you in when you were just a baby?"

"Yes, Aunt Meema," Sammy said.

"Remember the stories I told you about your real parents, Morris and Sara Kaminsky, and how they died during the influenza epidemic when you were barely a year old?"

Sammy nodded, his eyes wide. This conversation had nothing to do with Monk Westman.

"Your mother, she should rest in peace, was Sara Liebowitz before she married your father, Morris, who was my brother," Aunt Meema went on. "Sara, your mother, had a brother, Herman, your uncle, he should also rest in peace."

Sammy nodded dully. He knew little about his real parents, only what Aunt Meema had told him.

"Your Uncle Herman Liebowitz—your mother's older brother—had a daughter named Rose, who would be your first cousin. Do you understand me, Samuel?"

"I think so," Sammy said.

"Your Uncle Herman Liebowitz was not a well man," Aunt Meema continued. "Twenty years ago, he took his daughter Rose, who was maybe nine years old, and left New York. He thought the climate would be better for him somewhere else. Well, a Jew goes wherever he can make a living. In your Uncle Herman's case, it was a place called Arkansas. The last we heard, fourteen years ago, Uncle Herman had died, and nobody knew what became of your cousin Rose. She would have been fifteen at the time."

"She was twenty-eight at the time of her death," the tall man said.

Sammy looked at him, then to his Aunt Meema, then to his Uncle Jake. He was clearly confused.

"This is Mr. Tinkham, Sammy," Aunt Meema said, motioning to the tall man seated opposite him.

"Horace Tinkham," the man said. "From the Pinkerton Detective Agency, New York office. I've been trying to run you down for weeks."

"Me?" Sammy asked. He'd heard the word "detective" before. It usually had something to do with the police.

Tinkham said, "One month ago, we got a cable from our office in Kansas City. Seems a man by the name of John Slocum asked us to track you down. He's acting as the executor of your late cousin's estate."

Tinkham leaned closer to the table and looked directly at Sammy. "You're a rich man, Mr. Kaminsky."

"I am?" Sammy asked, wide-eyed.

Tinkham nodded. "Your late cousin left you assets that total more than one million dollars."

Aunt Meema gasped audibly. Uncle Jake murmured, "*Oy vey esmere!*"

Sammy blinked rapidly half a dozen times. He slowly reached across the table and plucked an onion roll from the bread basket. He nibbled it slowly, almost dreamily.

He tried to swallow, with no success. His throat felt tighter than the A-string on his violin.

"A million dollars, did you say?" Sammy said, his voice cracking in mid-sentence.

Tinkham nodded.

Sammy felt the blood rush up to his head, and suddenly he was dizzy. He didn't know whether to scream or faint.

He chose the latter.

"You'll forgive me," Sammy said to Tinkham. "But I think I don't feel so good."

"It wasn't any easier for me to believe, either," Tinkham said, as Sammy toppled off the chair and rolled up into a little ball on the floor.

The diners scarcely noticed, eating and screaming at one another as usual, spraying sour cream into one another's faces. Max the waiter stormed out of the kitchen, carrying a tray of food, and neatly stepped over Sammy's inert form on the floor as he delivered the kosher goodies to a table of bearded men in long black coats.

"A fine place to take a nap" was all Max said. "*Meshuga* kid."

4

"Is Texas anywhere near New Jersey?" Uncle Jake asked.

"Hush, Jake," Aunt Meema said, dipping the cloth into a pot of cold water. She squeezed it out and placed the cold towel on Sammy's forehead. He lay on a table in the kitchen, surrounded by cabbages and onions. Aunt Meema grabbed a dozen tablecloths and covered her nephew with them. She balled up a few more to use as a pillow.

Sammy moaned deeply, coming around. His eyes fluttered open.

"There, there," Aunt Meema said comfortingly, stroking his cheek affectionately. "Everything is fine."

Sammy opened his eyes. The first thing he saw was Lazlo the cook slicing a smoked salmon. He sat up abruptly, and Aunt Meema and Uncle Jake each grabbed him by a shoulder.

"You rest now, Samuel," Aunt Meema said, easing him back down gently and covering him with the tablecloths.

"You're a good boy," Uncle Jake said. "God is smiling on you."

"Hush, Jake," Aunt Meema said.

"I had the strangest dream," Sammy said. "A tall man came in and gave me a million dollars. I don't remember the rest . . . but you were there, Aunt Meema. And you, Uncle Jake . . ."

"*Oy,* mine darling Sammy," Aunt Meema said, mopping his brow with the cool cloth. "What you had was not a dream."

"It wasn't?" Sammy asked.

"You bet your *tuchas* it wasn't," Uncle Jake interjected.

Sammy sat up abruptly, and got dizzy again. He lay back down, but not before he saw, through the swinging kitchen doors, Mr. Tinkham sitting at a table and *noshing* on a plate of potato dumplings and sour cream.

"I'm sorry, Samuel," Aunt Meema said, dipping the cloth into the cold water again. "We should have told you."

"Told me what, Aunt Meema?" Sammy asked.

"Your uncle and myself, we knew about this cousin Rose Liebowitz of yours," Aunt Meema said, wiping Sammy's brow again. "We never saw the need to tell you about her." Aunt Meema then whispered into Sammy's ear, "Your cousin Rose was a lady of the evening."

"Does that mean she slept during the day?" Sammy asked, having no idea what his aunt was talking about.

"I suppose you could say that," Aunt Meema said.

"We never knew she was so rich," Uncle Jake responded. "A million dollars I couldn't make in ten lifetimes." He shook his head in wonderment.

"Jake," Aunt Meema snapped. "Get back to the cash register before Max steals us blind."

Uncle Jake ambled back into the dining room to relieve Max the waiter at the register. Max was a good waiter, but less than honest. He was famous for swiping other waiters' tips when their backs were turned.

Inside the kitchen, Aunt Meema continued wiping Sammy's brow with the cool cloth, trying to soothe him. Sammy was having none of it. The fifty cents a week he gave Professor Stossel seemed like a small fortune. In a neighborhood where earning forty dollars a month was the norm, Sammy could hardly conceive of a million.

"A million dollars," he muttered. "That's one thousand times one thousand."

"It isn't so simple," Aunt Meema said. "I was talking to that Mr. Tinkham, and . . . well, Sammy, I think you better go home and lie down a little. Your Uncle Jake and me, we'll close up early and come as soon as we can."

Aunt Meema helped her nephew up off the table and gently guided him out the door past Tinkham, who was mopping up some sour cream with a chunk of *challah* bread. Tinkham nodded to Aunt Meema, who nodded back. Sammy kept muttering about a million dollars.

He walked home in a daze, forgetting to take his violin, and went straight to bed.

Sammy woke up in his bed and looked around. He could see through the tenement window that it was dark outside. Since he never took naps, he awakened disoriented. He could hear the street sounds of the early evening; trolley car bells ringing, wagons clopping over the cobblestone streets, and Mr. and Mrs. Epstein in the next apartment screaming Yiddish curses at each other. Sammy judged the time to be about eight in the evening. Then it all came back to him.

He sat up and heard Aunt Meema and Uncle Jake talking in the living room. Then he heard a third person, a stranger, say something. He got up out of bed and padded a little unsteadily into the living room. Sitting on the couch were Aunt Meema and Uncle Jake. Across from them on a tattered chair, Mr. Tinkham the detective was sipping tea.

They all looked up as Sammy came in. Uncle Jake said, "Well there he is, mine little Corny Vanderbilt."

Aunt Meema said, "Sammy, you must be hungry. How about some nice baked chicken and a glass of tea?"

Sammy ignored her and walked up to Tinkham. He said, "Is it still true what you said, sir, about me being a millionaire?"

Uncle Jake said, "For God's sake, Sammy, how many times do you have to hear it?"

"Hush, Jake," Aunt Meema said.

Tinkham leaned over and put his teacup down onto the scarred coffee table. "I said you *inherited* holdings worth a million dollars. Collecting it is another story altogether."

Sammy looked at Aunt Meema quizzically. It still wasn't sinking in. His head felt funny, like it was filled with fog and old chewing gum.

"How old are you, son?" Tinkham asked.

"Twenty years old, next March," Sammy said.

"You ever been out of this neighborhood?" Tinkham said, already knowing the answer.

"I went to Coney Island once," Sammy said.

"I mean, have you ever been out of the state?" Tinkham asked pointedly.

Sammy thought about it. He said, "To speak God's truth, I haven't. Why?"

"I think you better sit down, Sammy," Aunt Meema said, her brow furrowed. "Sit, sweetheart."

Sammy grabbed a rickety wooden chair from the dining room table and sat.

Tinkham said, "Sammy, nobody's coming to your door and handing you a million dollars in a shitload of shoe boxes. Your cousin's assets are tied up in all kinds of things, like land, and ranches, small businesses. The money's not going to come to you, son. You have to go where *it* is."

"And where is it, Mr. Tinkham?" Sammy asked.

"The state of Texas," Tinkham said. "A long way from Coney Island."

"Where is this . . . Texas?" Sammy wanted to know. "Is it far?"

"Depends on your definition of far," Tinkham said.

"Yours will do nicely," Sammy said, trying to shake his head clear. His world had been suddenly turned upside down, and righting it was a chore indeed.

"Two thousand miles to the west, and then some," Tinkham said, reaching into the pocket of his jacket. "I've taken the liberty of bringing a map of the entire United States of America, to give you some idea."

Tinkham unfolded the map on the coffee table. He produced a pencil from his vest pocket and drew a line across the map, from New York all the way to West Texas. Sammy stared down at the map with wide eyes. Aunt Meema and Uncle Jake were similarly impressed. Their knowledge of the land beyond Brooklyn was as limited as their nephew's. Both were second-generation Americans, their parents having emigrated from Eastern Europe sixty years earlier.

"Starting here," Tinkham said, tapping New York with the tip of the pencil, "you'll need to travel west to Chicago, then down to Kansas City, then across to Dodge, then more trains down to Amarillo here, then from there a bunch of other trains to a bunch of whistle stops after that. To be honest, there's a dozen or more different railroads down around there. What you need to do, Sammy," Tinkham went on, "is get yourself to Killeen. That's where John Slocum will be waiting, to take you to Roseville."

"How will he know me?" Sammy asked.

Tinkham gave the tall, scrawny young man a quick up-and-down look.

"He'll know you, don't worry," Tinkham said.

"And just who is this Mr. John Slocum, anyway?" Aunt Meema piped up suspiciously. "Is he an *mensch,* a man of honor, or just some bum off the street?"

"That's a very good question, Meema," Uncle Jake said sagely.

"I mean, what do we know from this Texas place?" she asked. "We read in the newspaper about what happened to that Mr. Custer gentleman in that other place out west, that big Little Horn. Indians he had, *oy gevalt,* till they were coming out his *tuchas*! Better we should send our nephew back to the old country and the butchering Cossacks!"

"Never been to Texas myself," Tinkham said, "but as far as Indians go, I don't think you have to worry. The Army wiped out most of the dangerous ones, like the bushwhackin' Apache and the Comanche, some years back. As for the honesty of this John Slocum, my associates in Austin can personally vouch for his integrity. Sort of a legend in the West, or so they tell me. All I know is, if there was a million dollars waiting for me anywhere, much less Texas, you wouldn't see my coattails for the dust."

"Killing, whacking bushes, Indians, all kinds of crazy nonsense," Aunt Meema griped, waving her hands wildly. "This my nephew needs like a hole in the head."

She grabbed Sammy and locked him in a bear-hug embrace. His face was buried in her mammoth bosom, nearly suffocating him.

"Forget this foolishness, Samuel," she said. "You don't know *bupkus* from this Texas. Can you buy a decent bagel there? Are there any Jews in Texas? A synagogue? Better you should stay in Brooklyn with us. For what do you need trouble?"

"Meema," Uncle Jake put in. "A million dollars!"

"Million, *shmillion*," Aunt Meema declared. "I wouldn't care if it was a thousand. My nephew is not going to any Texas to maybe, God forbid, get himself killed. The answer is no!"

"For God's sake, Meema," Uncle Jake said. "Your nephew is almost twenty years old, he should decide for himself."

Aunt Meema looked Sammy square in the eye. He fought to meet her gaze. She said, "Samuel, you don't want to go so far away from home, thousands of miles from the ones who love you, to God only knows what. Sure, maybe there's some money, but you can't spend when you're dead." She turned to the Pinkerton man and said, "Don't you agree, Mr. Tinkham?"

"It's not for me to say, ma'am," Tinkham said, grabbing his bowler hat from the coatrack and jamming it on his head. "My job was to find your nephew and supply him with the information that was given to me. What he does after that is his business."

Tinkham made his way to the door and opened it. He said, "A million dollars is a lot of money, and there's a lot of dangerous men in Texas who'd like to get their hands on it. You'll probably have to fight, but what the hell, that's what America's really about, isn't it? If you decide to try for it, you'll need two things."

"What two things are that?" Sammy asked timidly.

"Courage, for one," Tinkham said. "Lots of it. And something else."

Sammy nodded expectantly.

"John Slocum," Tinkham said.

"All right," Sammy said. He was starting to feel sick again.

Tinkham motioned to the map spread out on the coffee table. "You can keep the map, son," he said. "And best of luck to you. May the Good Lord drop whatever He's doing and look after you."

Tinkham closed the door behind him. Sammy stood there, listening to the Pinkerton man's footsteps fade as he disappeared down the staircase.

There was a moment of silence.

"*Oy,*" Aunt Meema squeaked.

5

Sammy sat on the fire escape, listening to the sounds of the neighborhood winding down for the night. It was a little after midnight. Sleep would not come. A mild breeze swept through the tenement alleys of Williamsburg.

Up until five hours ago, Sammy's days had been filled with contented predictability: working at the restaurant, violin lessons with Professor Stossel, practicing those lessons, more work at the restaurant, sleep, and then more of the same. Occasionally Sophie the matchmaker, a fat, overbearing woman who smelled of cheap perfume, would come to the house and announce that she had "the perfect woman for your handsome nephew." Sammy never seemed to seek out available women on his own. He was the shyest boy in Williamsburg, Aunt Meema knew. Inevitably, she always agreed to Sophie the matchmaker's latest attempt to marry her nephew off.

Sammy sighed, thinking about it. The women Sophie knew were usually fat or ugly or both. Their fathers were always a little too eager to marry them off to anyone who was male and breathing.

Sammy had had a few crushes. There was Masha Turetsky, the rabbi's daughter. Masha, though, was in love with Bromberg the butcher's son Moishe, who wrote poetry. Then there had been Sophie Katzman, a freckle-faced redhead who'd been run over by a trolley when they were both fifteen.

While most of Sammy's male acquaintances had married or at the very least possessed firsthand knowledge of the female anatomy, Sammy had never been with a woman, in the biblical sense. Sex was what his aunt and uncle were doing sometimes on Sunday mornings when the bedsprings in their room next to his squeaked louder than usual.

Life, Sammy often thought, was passing him by. Life was something other people did, while he was but a bystander.

Presently, Uncle Jake padded into the living room, clad in baggy pajamas and a baggy bathrobe. His gray hair was all tousled. He saw his nephew sitting on the fire escape. He yawned and scratched his balls.

"Room for two out there?" Uncle Jake asked.

Sammy shrugged. "Sure," he said.

Uncle Jake climbed out onto the fire escape and sat opposite his nephew. He looked around at the tenement windows that surrounded them and down at the alley cats foraging for mice and food scraps.

"As breezes go," Uncle Jake commented, feeling the wind in what was left of his hair, "this one is nice."

"I guess," Sammy said.

Uncle Jake looked at Sammy, his only flesh and blood. Meema had never been able to carry a child to term; this they had found out the hard way, three times.

"So my little millionaire has something on his mind, I can tell," Uncle Jake said.

"Wouldn't you, Uncle Jake?" Sammy asked.

"Do you want to go?" Uncle Jake said. "To this Texas place?"

"I do and I don't," Sammy said. "It sounds exciting and different and maybe a little dangerous."

"Dangerous is not good," Uncle Jake said.

"No," Sammy said, "but dangerous is something I'm kind of used to."

"You mean Monk Westman?" Uncle Jake asked. "How he makes you play on your violin for him all the time?"

"How did you know about that?" Sammy asked his uncle incredulously. "I never told you or Aunt Meema."

"It's a small neighborhood, smaller than you think," Uncle Jake said. "People hear things, they tell me. I hear things, I tell them. Life is a circle, Sammy."

"From neighborhoods I know. That's not what scares me."

"So what scares you?" Uncle Jake asked.

Sammy, who'd taken his violin out on the fire escape with him, picked it up and started tightening the strings.

"What I don't know scares me," Sammy said. "The world out there, the one past the river, I don't know from. Like Aunt Meema said, God only knows what lies ahead. Still, a million dollars . . ."

Uncle Jake rubbed his chin thoughtfully. He said, "Sammy, my grandfather used to say, 'Fate doesn't come knocking on your door every day, so when he does, don't be a *putz*. Let him in.' Sammy, fate just paid you a visit today. You need to decide if you want to let him in or not."

"And if I don't," Sammy said, "does that mean I'm a *putz*?"

"To be perfectly honest," Uncle Jake said, "the answer is a definite maybe. I'm not you, you're not me. Listen to your heart, nephew."

"What if I can't hear my heart so well?" Sammy asked weakly. He'd never been so confused in his whole life.

"The heart never lies, so you'll hear it sooner or later," Uncle Jake said. "And if you try not to hear it, you'll hear it anyway. Your ancestors, Sammy, came to America from the old country with empty pockets. They were scared, too, nephew, for weeks huddled into a smelly hold in a ship. They came with nothing but the clothes on their backs and the dream of a better life. Sometimes a person has to take chances, Sammy, see what's on the other side of that ocean."

"I don't know," Sammy said doubtfully. "Aunt Meema—"

"Meema, *Shmeema*," Uncle Jake snorted. "Your aunt loves you, Sammy, but that doesn't mean she knows what's best for you, God bless her. Oh, no. Only *you* know what's best for you."

"I'm not so sure I do," Sammy said.

"Sammy, look at it this way," Uncle Jake said, pointing a crooked forefinger an inch from the tip of Sammy's nose. "If you stay in Brooklyn, what do you have to look forward to? Slaving your days away over a hot restaurant. Waiting for Sophie the matchmaker to find you a woman who doesn't make your stomach turn over? Working your fingers to the bone for pennies, sucking in this dirty air, living your days in three crowded tenement rooms, dreaming of something better until those dreams fall away one by one like the hairs on your head?"

Texas. The West. Sammy had visions of marauding redskins and barking guns in barrooms, of a world which he could barely comprehend, one he knew nothing about.

"But Aunt Meema," Sammy said hoarsely.

"Between you and me, another excellent reason to leave," Uncle Jake said.

"You think I should go?" Sammy said, a glimmer of hope sprouting in his belly.

"Not exactly," Uncle Jake said. "I just think you'd be a fool if you didn't."

With that, Uncle Jake crawled back through the window into the living room. He nodded his head toward the kitchen.

"Come to the kitchen," he said to his nephew. "Your Aunt Meema made some chopped liver. The way you like it, with onions."

Sammy said, "Why not?"

Sammy told Aunt Meema of his decision the next morning. He was going.

Aunt Meema's reaction, not surprisingly, was negative and then some. She screamed and hollered and carried on, telling her nephew that if he went to Texas, he'd come back in a week—in a coffin. Besides, she argued, the train fare that far away would cost a fortune, money they didn't have.

An hour later, a Western Union messenger boy came with a telegram addressed to Samuel D. Kaminsky of Brooklyn.

It read: "Railroad tickets to Chicago, Amarillo, and Killeen waiting for you with stationmaster at Grand Central, New York City STOP. Have arranged a bank transfer for $200 at bank, traveling money STOP. Will meet you 18 April in Killeen, five P.M. STOP. John Slocum. Roseville, Texas STOP."

"I said it before, and I'll say it now," Aunt Meema bellowed at her nephew. "You're not going thousands of miles way!" She stomped into the kitchen and slammed the door behind her, then poked her head out of the door. "You want me maybe to have heart attacks worrying over you? Is that what you want, Samuel, to kill your Aunt Meema with grief? The woman who raised you, fed you, wiped your runny nose, your little *tuchas*? The woman who took you to heart? Is this what you want, Samuel? I should go to my coffin worrying?"

She slammed the kitchen door again, followed by the loud sounds of banging pots and pans.

"I think," Uncle Jake said to Sammy, "it would be wise if you started packing."

Aunt Meema blubbered shamelessly, crying into a handkerchief, attracting the attention of seemingly every soul in Grand Central Station. Sammy shifted the cheap cardboard suitcase from one hand to the other. His violin was tucked under one arm. The suitcase contained every article of clothing he owned, plus two pairs of worn-out shoes with holes in the bottoms. He'd never gotten around to taking them to Bloom the shoemaker to get them resoled.

"Texas he goes," Aunt Meema wailed. "Weeds that tumble, people with guns." She was clutching a huge greasy paper bag filled with a week's worth of salami sandwiches and bananas more black than yellow. "Everything they eat out there is from pork. Promise me you won't eat any pork, Samuel."

Uncle Jake had gone to the stationmaster's office to pick up Sammy's train tickets and had yet to return. The first lap of his journey would take Sammy to Chicago. The train was scheduled to leave in less than ten minutes.

"I read the English newspapers. Indians they got there," Aunt Meema said. "Sitting Horse, Crazy Bull. What kind of names is that for people?"

"I'll be back as soon as I can, Aunt Meema," Sammy said. "And when I am, we'll all be rich. You and Uncle Jake won't have to work sixteen hours a day in that restaurant."

"Your cousin Rose, she should rest in peace, didn't die from a mosquito bite," Aunt Meema said. "She was shot to death, Sammy, and that's what you have to look forward to if you get on that train."

"Aunt Meema," Sammy said, putting down the suitcase and violin case. "Fate only knocks on your door once a night. If you're a *putz*, you let him in."

"You sound like your uncle," Aunt Meema said, tears streaming down her face.

Uncle Jake appeared out of the throng of travelers, clutching Sammy's tickets. He was also carrying something in a paper bag.

Uncle Jake pushed his way through the crowd and grinned broadly as he handed his nephew the train tickets. "My little *pisher* is going west. I can hardly believe it."

"Hush, Jake," Aunt Meema snapped.

"I got you this," Uncle Jake said, thrusting the package at Sammy. "A little present for going away."

Inside the bag was a book called *A Texas Cow Boy, or, Fifteen Years on the Hurricane Deck of a Spanish Pony*. The book was written was by someone called Chas A.

Siringo, "an old stove-up 'cow puncher' who has spent nearly twenty years on the Great Western Cattle Ranges." On the front of a book was an illustration of the author, a short, cocky-looking man wearing a big black hat. He was leaning against a wall. He had a knife sheathed on his belt and was gripping the barrels of a rifle that was almost as tall as he was. He didn't look mean, exactly, but neither did he look like a man Aunt Meema would want to have over for *Hanukkah* dinner.

"What the hell," Uncle Jake said, pointing at the cover illustration. "If that little *nudnik* can punch a cow, so can you."

Then, much like the Red Sea, the crowd in the huge train station parted, amid nervous murmurs. Monk Westman, looking like a slightly deformed Moses without the beard, came walking up to Sammy. On his heels were half a dozen of his toughest, meanest-looking associates, including Ratface Cohen and Dizzy Izzy Farkus. Westman gave Aunt Meema and Uncle Jake no more than a cursory glance and said to Sammy, "I heard you're going away."

"Uh . . . just for a little while," Sammy stammered.

"So you couldn't tell me yourself?" Monk asked indignantly. "I had to hear it from strangers?"

"I meant to tell you," Sammy said sheepishly. "It was a little sudden."

Aunt Meema and Uncle Jake said nothing. They knew this Monk Westman, the most feared man in Williamsburg. The restaurant was the only business on the block that Monk didn't extort money from, thanks to Sammy and his violin. Now that Sammy was leaving, Uncle Jake wondered dimly, would that arrangement change?

"I'd like to borrow Sammy for a minute," Monk said, more as a statement than a request. He took Sammy gently by the arm and led him away from the crowd. Sammy's knees knocked together. A mad Monk was a bad Monk.

"This Texas you're going to," Monk said. "How far is it? Do you have to cross an ocean?"

"No," Sammy said. "Just the Hudson River."

"That far?"

Monk started pacing back and forth. "I don't know anything about this Texas joint," he said. "But how bad could it be? Worse than the Bowery? Nah." He turned to Sammy. "I don't know what it is, but I got a bug up my ass about you, Sammy. You and that violin brought a little pleasure into a life that has none. Believe me, it's not easy being the meanest man in Brooklyn. I just want to say, Sammy—and I don't say this to everyone—if you should get in over your head, if your back is ever up against a wall, give me a holler or two. Maybe I can help. I don't know how far away this Texas is, but how far can it be?"

"Close to three thousand miles," Sammy murmured.

"Don't worry about your family," Monk said, motioning to Uncle Jake and Aunt Meema. "I'll keep an eye on 'em."

"Thank you," Sammy said.

"All aboard for the Limited to Chicago," a voice boomed through the cavernous train station. "Track nine, departing in five minutes."

"Well, I guess I'll see you around, Monk," Sammy said.

Monk gave Sammy an affectionate punch on the arm; the kind of affectionate punch that causes two-inch ugly purple bruises. Sammy winced, but Monk took no notice. He said, "Remember, kid. You get in a jam, Monk is here to help."

With that, Monk turned and walked away, his partners-in-crime following dutifully one step behind him.

"If those are the kind of people our nephew's associating with, maybe it's good he's going away," Uncle Jake said.

"Shut up, Jake," Aunt Meema said. She ran to her nephew and swept him into her arms again, crushing him.

"You don't have to go, Sammy," she wailed. "It's not too late. We could go home now, and I could make us some nice lunch, and—"

"Hush, Meema," Uncle Jake said, asserting himself for perhaps the first time in the history of their thirty-year marriage. He tore Sammy from his wife's beefy arms. "He's a man now, Meema. Leave him be."

Uncle Jake handed Sammy his battered suitcase and the bag of salami sandwiches and bananas. Grease had now thoroughly soaked the thick brown paper.

"God is with you, Sammy," Uncle Jake said. "Of that I'm certain. But remember, nephew: We'll always be here for you, if you decide this Texas place doesn't agree with you."

"Thank you, Uncle Jake," Sammy said, and to his amazement, Uncle Jake threw his arms around him and gave him a hug, something Sammy could not recall him ever doing, not even the day he was *bar mitzvahed*. Behind them, Aunt Meema continued crying.

Sammy broke from his uncle's embrace and starting walking toward the gate to track 9. He looked back once, and damn if Uncle Jake wasn't crying, too. Part of Sammy was tempted to turn around and head straight back to the security of Brooklyn, but he kept going nonetheless, some unseen force propelling him forward to whatever fate had in store for him. He was scared, but he also felt a kind of euphoria that made his heart race. Someting big was around the corner, Sammy knew. Good or bad, he didn't know. Suddenly, he had to pee something awful.

6

Slocum sloshed some whiskey into the shot glass, mostly missing, but still managing to get an ounce or so of Solly Conklin's liquid dynamite into it. Slocum downed it in one gulp and tried to pour another. He missed the glass completely this time, by a good six inches, and succeeded only in pouring the rotgut into his lap.

He was sitting at a table in Conklin's saloon—or Rose's saloon; one of the three she'd owned and Conklin managed. It was about ten in the morning, the third day into Slocum's nonstop, 120-proof, memory-melting, brain-pickling, liver-rotting, all-out bender. He'd been drinking steadily for close to fifty-eight hours, setting a new record for himself. His last binge, some six years earlier—which had occurred after he'd been forced to shoot his beloved horse Moonbeam when the mare had broken a leg—had lasted two days. The hangover had lasted four. Still, as much as Slocum had loved Moonbeam, he'd never made love to him, which was where the chestnut and Rose Liebowitz parted company.

No amount of cheap liquor, though, could erase the memory of his beloved Rose.

Next to the table, a short, chubby Negro man was pounding gleefully on the piano. The stub of a cheroot was clenched in the corner of his mouth. He was wearing a stained white shirt, a tattered red vest, and a derby that was cocked low down on the right side of his bald head, almost over his eye. A glass of warm, flat beer sat atop the piano. He was performing, for the tenth time in a row, a little ditty called "You Meet the Nicest People in Your Dreams." Each rendition had been good for a dollar bill from Slocum. The song had been Rose's favorite.

After the song was over, Slocum threw another dollar bill in the piano player's direction and slurred, "Again, Mr. Botts."

"Yes, sir," the piano player chirped, and ripped into the tune once more.

His name was Abraham Lincoln Botts and he hailed from Meridian, Mississippi. He'd spent the last sixteen of his thirty years banging the ivories aboard the riverboats that traveled up and down the Big Muddy. He'd come west to Texas after incurring some heavy gambling debts in New Orleans—debts he couldn't pay if he worked for two hundred years. It seemed every saloon in Texas was starved for any kind of music, so work was plentiful.

Still, Texas was hostile territory for both man and beast. The cowboys who came to drink in Solly's saloon every Saturday night fired their guns into the ceiling and occasionally at Abe himself. Only last month, in a saloon in Stephensville, a drunken cowpoke had pumped four bullets into the floor around Abe's feet to make him play faster. Abraham Lincoln Botts had left for points west the next morning, and ended up in Roseville.

Miss Rose was a nice lady. She immediately put him to work in her whorehouse, the Roseville Happytime Emporium, and paid him well. On slow nights he moonlighted at Solly's Saloon. Mr. Conklin wasn't as nice as Miss Rose, who strictly forbade Conklin swiping Abe's tips. Abraham felt truly sad when she passed on.

When she died, he'd been thinking of continuing his trek to San Francisco, his ultimate destination. That city, Abe had heard over the years, was a boomtown. He'd stayed in Roseville for only one reason: Mr. Slocum had asked him to, promising him the same generous salary that Miss Rose had paid. And Roseville wasn't nearly as bad as some of the rowdy cow towns he'd worked in.

Abe ripped through the melody once more as Slocum attempted to pour another drink. He looked ready to topple from his chair and stretch out on the sawdust-covered floor, which Abe had been expecting him to do for the last hour. No one, Abe thought, could suck up as much hooch as Mr. Slocum had and still be sitting up. Then again, this Mr. Slocum seemed to be cut from a different cloth than most white men Abe had run into. He was actually fair and decent, even in the depths of his boozy mourning. Mr. Slocum was hurting bad from Miss Rose's death, Abe knew, and drinking would only make it worse.

"There's some things whiskey can't drown, Mr. John," Abe said, stroking the piano keys. "Sometimes, it evens makes the pain hurt more."

"No offense, Mr. Botts, but shut up and play," Slocum said drunkenly. He tried to pour another drink and instead slopped another slug straight onto his crotch.

"Shit," he muttered.

"Terrible waste of good whiskey, Mr. Slocum," Abe said.

"You're right," Slocum said, his eyes puffy pink slits. "You pour it."

"I'd rather pour you some coffee," Abe said, banging at the piano. He went into a different tune, "Camptown Races." Slocum didn't notice.

"I hate coffee," Slocum said, drinking straight from the bottle. It was much easier. He downed the last quarter of the hooch and belched loudly. "Another sottle, Bolly," Slocum called to the barkeep. "Make it a small one."

Solly rushed to accommodate Slocum's drunken request. Abe and Slocum both knew that Solly Conklin had been offered a half interest in the three saloons once Potter took over Roseville. Solly was more than willing to ply Slocum with whiskey and let the chips fall where they may.

Abe eyeballed the two tough hombres standing at the bar, both Eustace Potter's men. They were watching Slocum like hawks circling a jackrabbit. Solly rushed up carrying another bottle of whiskey, and set it down on the table. Before Slocum could grab it, however, a plump brown hand darted across the table and snatched the bottle up.

Slocum looked bleary-eyed over at Abe, who poured the whiskey into a nearby spittoon.

"And jus' what the hell are you doin' that for?" Slocum wanted to know.

"With all due respect, Mr. John," Abe said, "I'd say you've had enough. You got a couple of hungry buzzards waiting on your drunken ass over there at the bar, just itchin' to give you some grief."

Slocum turned and looked at the two men. They were kids, barely twenty, with bad attitudes and too much to prove. Slocum had seen them riding around town on Potter's heels. Slip Pomeroy and Whitey Watson, Slocum remembered through his booze-fogged brain.

Slocum knew that as long as he didn't collapse into an unconscious heap, he could take them. Let the bastards try, he thought. In his booze-addled mind, prairie trash such as them were as much responsible for Rose's death as anyone.

" 'Bout time you was leavin' for the train depot in Killeen, ain't it, Mr. John?" Abe asked, tickling the ivories. "The five o'clock train ought to be rollin' in shortly."

This was true, Slocum thought dimly. Rose's nephew was due to arrive that day. Slocum had already rented a rig from the livery to meet him.

"I do believe that's correct," Slocum said, and pulled a pocket watch from his vest. The hands on the watch—both sets of them; Slocum was seeing double—indicated that he had barely an hour to get there, and the trip to Killeen took at least two. He'd have to make serious haste.

Slocum straightened up, trying to stand erect. It was a challenge. He wobbled as if his legs were made of rubber.

He made his way unsteadily toward the batwing doors, jamming his hat on his head. As he passed by the bar, Slip Pomeroy stuck out his leg and tripped him. Slocum went sprawling onto the floor and flat on his face with a resounding thud. The smells of soggy sawdust and stale beer assaulted his nostrils.

"Looks like the big, bad lawman can't hold his whiskey," Pomeroy said, and he and Whitey Watson broke out in loud guffaws.

Slocum got to his feet unsteadily, spitting out sawdust and wiping it off his vest and pants.

"What's the matter, Slocum?" Whitey Watson said. "You all busted up 'cause your whore is pushin' up lilies?"

Slocum straightened up and faced the two young cowpunchers.

"I may be drunk," he said, "but shitheels like you sober me up real quick-like."

Their raucous laughter stopped abruptly. Pomeroy glared at Slocum, his right hand dropping down to his holster. His hard, chiseled face usually had a chilling effect on men twice Pomeroy's age. Slocum, though, was unimpressed.

"Looks like you boys could use a drink," Slocum said, and signed to the bartender. "Couple of sugartits for the babies, Solly. On me."

Pomeroy's eyes widened in rage, and he went for his gun. Like lightning, Slocum pointed two fingers and poked Pomeroy in the eyes, not gently. Pomeroy howled in pain, his hands flying up to his face. Before Whitey Watson could even react, Slocum lashed out with his left fist and smashed it into Watson's nose, crushing bone and cartilage. Whitey howled in pain. The two young men sounded like two coyotes mating at midnight. To add to their discomfort, Slocum grabbed each of them firmly by the sweetmeats and gave them a healthy squeeze. It was difficult to tell who was wailing in pain the loudest, Pomeroy or Watson.

Slocum gave their nuts another agonizing squeeze and released them. Each of them bent over painfully and sank to the barroom floor, clutching his groin.

"You boys need to learn to respect your elders a bit more," Slocum said.

Slocum dropped to his haunches and pulled out his Colt. He grabbed Pomeroy's right hand and pressed the little bastard's forefinger flat against the floor. Pomeroy was in too much pain to protest, having curled into a fetal position from the throbbing in his balls. Slocum smashed the butt of the Colt onto Pomeroy's forefinger three times, until he heard bone crunching and was satisfied the finger was sufficiently broken.

"Maybe now you'll think twice about reaching for a gun around me," Slocum said.

Slocum stood and finished dusting himself off. The other people in the saloon were quiet as mice, mesmerized by Slocum's display.

Abe said to Slocum, somewhat nervously, "Excuse me, Mr. John, but I do believe you broke the wrong finger. Man shoots with his right."

Slocum shook his head wearily. "Is that a fact?" he said.

Pomeroy lay whimpering on the floor. Slocum said to him, "Which way to the door, son?"

With his good hand, Pomeroy pointed with his forefinger toward the batwing doors. Slocum stomped on it. The sound of snapping bone echoed throughout the saloon. Pomeroy howled again.

"Are you happy now?" Slocum asked Abe, and left.

7

The girl sitting opposite him on the train, Sammy thought, reminded him a lot of Sadie Feinberg, the best-looking girl in Public School 179 on Knickerbocker Avenue. This girl was prettier, though. She had silky golden hair pinned up under a red bonnet to keep out the choking west Texas dust. She was wearing a stiffly starched green dress that showed just enough to her cleavage and round curves to take a man's mind off the scenery outside.

Sammy alternately glanced at her and looked away, not wanting to attract attention. For her part, the girl, who looked to be about eighteen or so, ignored Sammy completely. She read her book, *Great Expectations* by Charles Dickens, totally engrossed.

Sammy worked up his courage, clearing his throat. Having rehearsed in his mind a proper introductory remark for the last two hours, he was surprised by what came out.

"Nice weather we had tomorrow," he squeaked, despite his efforts not to.

She eyed him disdainfully, looking very much put upon, as though he were a fat horsefly buzzing around her ears. She said, "Yes. I heard yesterday's is supposed to be even nicer."

She returned to her book, leaving this odd-looking boy clutching what looked like a violin case to sink down in defeat.

Sammy stared out the window for a minute and took a deep breath, sucking up every last ounce of courage he could.

"Are you going to Killeen?" he asked, falling back on his reserve opening line.

The girl stole a glance at him, sighed, and went back to her reading. Sammy looked back out the window. This was not going well, but then, his previous efforts with the fairer sex had rarely ended in any kind of victory. Sammy simply felt tongue-tied and nervous around women.

He had been riding one train or another for the best part of a week now. Once you were past Chicago, the trains got less and less comfortable, velvet-lined seats being replaced by hard wooden ones. Edible food was harder to come by. Somewhere in the middle of Oklahoma, Aunt Meema's food bag long gone, Sammy had been forced to spend a dollar on some cold, hard, dough-wrapped meat pies called *tamales,* bought from some peddler at the station. As hungry as he was, Sammy's stomach had rebelled after he'd eaten the second one, and he barely made it to the lavatory before losing both of them completely.

The girl had gotten on in Fort Worth, where Sammy had also changed to yet another train, earlier that morning. By this time, Sammy's clothes were caked with alkali dust, and he was sweating profusely. The windows were closed; as hot as this made the train, he preferred it to the west Texas silt that clogged his throat when the windows were open. He felt like a dirty rag after days of train travel. Brooklyn in August wasn't nearly as hot as Texas in March.

Between starving half to death and not having anyone to talk to, Sammy missed Williamsburg more than ever. He wanted to go home. Somehow, though, he felt a compelling need to finish his journey and, like Uncle

Jake said, seek his destiny, whatever the hell it might prove to be.

This girl was the first human being he had spoken to in nearly six days. He'd read Mr. Charlie Siringo's book three times and had slept sitting up. His body was one big ache.

Despite everything, Sammy was strongly attracted to this girl.

"Only six months till Christmas," he said. He knew this to be a holiday non-Jews celebrated.

She flashed him a brief, indulgent smile but did not stop reading.

"Do you believe in Sandy Claws?" Sammy asked with a sad attempt at a chuckle.

This time, the pretty girl looked up and slammed her book shut on her lap.

"Were you addressing me?" she asked.

Sammy froze momentarily and stammered, "No. Of course not. No. I'm sorry. I . . . you . . . uh . . ."

Embarrassed, he averted his gaze and directed his stare out the window.

The girl finally went back to her book. As she read, she reached for a canvas bag that was sitting on the seat beside her. She opened it and pulled out a package wrapped in stained newspaper. Inside was a sandwich of some kind, cut into four parts. The girl daintily plucked one and started nibbling on it.

Three feet away, across from her, she could hear the young man's stomach rumble. She stole a quick glance at him. He was sort of cute in a gangly, awkward, boyish sort of way. He was tall and a little too thin for her tastes. At the same time, though, there was something about him that seemed fragile, like a glass figurine. His attempts to strike up a conversation with her were pathetic and endearing at the same time.

She held the sandwich out to him. "Would you care for part of my sandwich?" she asked. "It's watercress and butter."

It could have been mud and mustard, Sammy normally would have jumped at it. He knew, though, that it would be discourteous to accept her offer. A man never took food from a woman.

"No, thank you," Sammy said, eyeing the sandwich ravenously.

"It's okay, I have plenty for both of us," she said.

Sammy felt his saliva drooling out of his mouth and dribbling down his chin. He hadn't eaten in almost a day and a half. Still, he thought, Charlie Siringo, the stove-up Texas cowboy, wouldn't have taken the sandwich. Sammy wouldn't either.

"I ain't hungry," Sammy said. "Ain't" was a word Charlie Siringo used a lot.

The girl smiled now, and this time it was genuine. Munching on her dinner, she rummaged through her canvas bag and pulled out an apple.

"I have this apple I really don't want," she said. "Would you care for it?"

A little apple, Sammy reasoned, Charlie Siringo wouldn't have any problem accepting. Sammy took it gratefully and wolfed it down in four bites—core, seeds, and all.

"Thank you," he said with a loud belch.

"You're welcome," she said.

"Excuse me," Sammy said sheepishly. "It was rude of me."

She smiled a little. "My grandma used to say, 'If the Good Lord didn't want us to burp, He wouldn't have given us food.' "

She returned to her Dickens, munching daintily on her sandwich. Sammy knew this was a crucial moment. If he didn't sustain the conversation, it would fade away like yesterday's sunset.

"How far are you going?" Sammy asked. "On the train, I mean."

"Killeen," she said. "I was in Fort Worth visiting my aunt and uncle."

"Me, too," Sammy said.

They continued on in silence for a few moments. Then Sammy piped up with "My name is Samuel David Kaminsky from Brooklyn, New York."

"My name is Emily Louisa Shields," she said. "From Roseville, Texas."

"Roseville?" he asked. "You live in Roseville? That's where I'm going. Maybe we'll run into each other."

"I don't think that would be proper, Mr. Kaminsky," Emily said. "I am, after all, engaged to be married."

Sammy's heart sank like a hunk of lead in the Atlantic. His face reddened and he felt a hot flush.

"What brings you all the way to Roseville?" Emily asked.

Sammy had lost his appetite for this conversation, but said, "My cousin Rose died and left me some money and things."

"Rose Liebowitz?" Emily asked. "She was your cousin?"

"That's right," Sammy said.

"We heard some of her kin was coming to claim her inheritance," Emily said. "I thought . . . that is . . . we thought . . . I mean . . . we were expecting, well—"

"Expecting what?" Sammy said.

"Um . . . well, someone, you know, tough like Miss Rose."

"Tough?" Sammy asked.

"You know," Emily went on. "Texas tough. Miss Rose, she was hard as a horseshoe nail. We just figured any of her kin . . ." Her voice trailed off. Emily realized she was more than likely speaking too much of her mind, which, as her mother and father constantly reminded her, she was wont to do. "I'm sorry," she said. "I didn't mean to—"

Sammy's ears started getting hot. "It's all right," he said.

"I didn't know Miss Rose really," Emily said. "But Papa always spoke kindly of her. He said she would have made an excellent man, except she was too pretty."

"I never actually met her," Sammy said. He wished he was in another state, so humiliated he felt. "I didn't even know she existed until a week ago." He hoped Roseville was twice the size of Brooklyn so that he'd never see this girl again. Judging from the size of some of the Texas towns he'd passed through, however, Sammy doubted it. He'd been eager to learn more about his cousin Rose, but Emily had taken the wind of those sails.

Mercifully, the conductor, a short, squat elf of a man, sauntered down the aisle of the passenger car looking at a stopwatch. "Killeen, Texas, next station stop in five minutes. Killeen, Texas, next station stop."

Sammy instantly stood and started reaching up to the luggage rack for his cardboard suitcase, which after five days of negligent baggage handlers and Pullman porters, was nearly in tatters. Emily likewise stood, but made no effort to reach for her suitcase.

"If you'd be so kind, Mr. Kaminsky, to get my bag for me," she said, hoping to patch his male pride, which she had so thoughtlessly bruised. She couldn't help it. He was kind of cute, but he was as thin as a slice of bacon and looked as fragile as a china teacup.

Sammy nodded graciously and grabbed her suitcase with both hands. At the same instant, the train lurched, slowing down. Sammy tumbled backward, still clutching Emily's suitcase, and landed flat in the lap of an obese woman, who started wailing for the conductor. Sammy scrambled to his feet, thoroughly flustered.

Grunting, Sammy handed Emily the suitcase, which seemed to weigh a ton, as the train rolled to a stop. She carried it effortlessly down the aisle. Sammy had never met a girl who was stronger than most men he knew and still pretty.

They disembarked. Waiting at the station beside a horse and buckboard wagon was a tall, stout man wearing worn overalls and a battered cowboy hat, just like the one Charlie Siringo wore. He had a big, bushy salt-and-pepper beard, which made him look, to Sammy, like a rabbi with muscles.

Emily dropped her suitcase, ran to the man, and threw her arms around him.

"Papa," she cried. "Oh, Papa, it's good to see you."

"Welcome home, daughter," the big man said with affection, and hugged her back. "You're lookin' more purty every day."

"Where's Mama?" Emily asked.

"Back to the ranch, cookin' up a storm," the big man said. "But your brothers ought to be along shortly. Luke, too."

"Luke's coming?" Sammy heard Emily say, and she didn't sound totally happy about by this news.

The train started to pull away. When it slowly chugged out of the station, Sammy walked cautiously over to Emily and her father.

"Excuse me," he said, and held out Emily's book. "You left Mr. Dickens on your seat."

"Oh, thank you, Mr. Kaminsky," Emily said with a smile that melted his heart. "That was very kind of you." She turned to her father. "Papa, this is Samuel David Kaminsky from New York City. Samuel, this is my father, Stanley Shields."

Mr. Shields eyed this skinny Yankee suspiciously. Sammy extended his hand. When Emily's father didn't take it, Sammy, not knowing what else to do with it, awkwardly brushed his hair.

"He's kin to Miss Rose," Emily added.

Mr. Shields's sun-weathered face broke into a grin.

"Kin to Miss Rose, you say? Well, that's a horse of a different color, yes, sir." He grabbed Sammy's hand and pumped it vigorously, almost yanking his arm from the socket.

"A fine woman, for a Yankee," he said approvingly. "Could have foreclosed the mortgage on our spread anytime she wanted to, what with times bein' tough. Wouldn't let that other sidewindin' buzzard what owns t'other half of the bank do it. Saved this town from the likes of the Fisher Gang, too. Got the poor woman killed." Mr. Shields took off his hat in respect. "It's a pleasure to meet you, son."

"Likewise, I'm sure," Sammy said. "You wouldn't happen to know a Mr. John Slocum, would you? He was supposed to meet me here." He took off his hat and wiped his brow. "It sure is hot in Texas."

"Best get used to it, boy," Mr. Shields. "West Texas can get hotter than the bowels of hell sometimes."

"Papa!" Emily gasped, shocked.

"Sure, I know old Slocum," Mr. Shields said. "But you best not be waitin' for him to show. Heard he crawled inside a whiskey bottle a few days back and ain't crawled out yet. You best come with us, son. Be happy to drop you off in town. Better still, y'all are welcome to come back with us to the Bar-S. The missus is whippin' us up a feast. Chicken and dumplings with all the trimmin's."

"We'd be delighted to have you, Mr. Kaminsky," Emily said. "Mama's an excellent cook."

She was interrupted by three men on horseback galloping toward the station. Upon closer examination, they all appeared to be about Sammy's age. They were rugged men raised on the harsh west Texas country. With their checkered flannel shirts and dust-coated, sunbaked faces, they could have been chisled out of the landscape.

They rode up and dismounted. All three seemed impossibly tall and lean as they ran to Emily, whooping and hollering louder than a Knickerbocker Avenue fish peddler. She embraced one of them.

"Billy," Emily said affectionately. "I go away for three weeks and you grow six inches."

"You're loco, Emmie," the one called Billy said, hugging her back. "Ain't never heard such, little sister."

Emily broke away from Billy and embraced the second tall man, who was probably another of her brothers. Sammy was momentarily forgotten as Emily gleefully greeted them.

"I swear, Elmer," Emily said, hugging him. "You're a sight for sore eyes."

Sammy didn't miss the fact that she hugged the third man with noticeably less enthusiasm. He didn't seem to notice, though, sweeping Emily up in his powerful arms and giving her a passionate kiss. Emily broke it off quickly.

"You're looking real fine, Emmie," he said. Sammy could see that the guy was head over heels in love with her.

"Oh, Luke," she said, her smile faltering. She smoothed her ruffled dress, seemingly eager to be away from his grasp. "How are you?"

"Better, honey, now that you're back home where you belong," Luke said.

Stanley Shields piped up. "We best be gettin' along. Know how your mama gets when we're late for vittles." He started to move toward the buckboard.

"Just a second, Papa," Emily said. She turned to Sammy and said, "Samuel, these are my brothers, Billy and Elmer. Billy, Elmer, this is Samuel Kaminsky from New York."

Emily's brothers regarded Sammy as they would a fly on a windowsill, their faces blank. Emily said, "And this is Luke Price, my fian—"

The one named Luke glared at Sammy. He eased Emily aside, gently but firmly, and strolled over to Sammy. Sammy had to bend his neck to look up at Luke, who towered over him like a live oak.

There was rage in Luke's ink-black eyes. "Do Ah know you?" he drawled.

"Uh . . . no, I don't believe we ever met," Sammy stammered, his throat dryer than a tenement brick. "My name is—"

"I heared your name," he said. "You messin' with mah lady?"

"I beg your pardon?" Sammy asked, genuinely confused by Luke's vocabulary. "Could you maybe repeat that in English?"

Luke looked disdainfully at the violin case tucked under Sammy's left arm. "What the hell's that?"

"This?" Sammy asked, opening the violin case nervously and showing Luke the instrument. "It's a violin."

"Looks like a damn fiddle to me," Luke said sharply, his eyes narrowed suspiciously. "You plan on fiddlin' with mah woman?"

Sammy had no idea what this person was talking about, but he was smart enough to realize that this Luke was itching for a fight. Luke wasn't half as tough as Monk Westman, Sammy thought, but he looked capable nonetheless of ripping Sammy into even-size chunks.

"I don't know exactly what you—" Sammy started.

He said no more. Luke lashed out and punched him squarely on the jaw. Sammy's head snapped backward like the cap off a bottle of sarsaparilla, the violin case flying. His eyeballs rolled up into his head and he fell into the dirt, flat on his back.

"Luke!" Emily cried, and ran to Sammy, who was shaking his head dizzily. Before she could even kneel down beside him, Luke pushed her away brusquely and stood over Sammy. Emily's brothers tittered.

Luke waited for Sammy to stand shakily. Blood trickled from the corner of his mouth. Sammy said, "I seem to have made you angry, Mr. Pri—"

Luke lashed out again and slugged Sammy squarely in the right eye. Sammy crashed to the ground once more. He struggled again to his feet.

There was pure hate in Luke's eyes as he delivered a hard blow into Sammy's midsection. The breath rushed out of Sammy's lungs and he dropped to his knees, gasping for breath. Emily angrily grabbed Luke from behind with an angry cry, but he shook her off like a pesky mosquito.

"Papa," Emily pleaded, "make him stop."

The elder Shields said, "Hush, girl, this is between them two boys." Her brothers continued tittering.

Sammy, on his hands and knees, tried sucking in some air, his face the color of new cheese.

Luke kicked Sammy in the side, sending him sprawling into the dirt. He pressed his boot against Sammy's chest, pinning him flat against the ground.

"Mess with my woman again, you Yankee bastard, and I'll rip your gizzard out," Luke warned.

He turned and grabbed Emily by the arm, leading her toward the wagon. Emily chose not to protest too much. It would, she knew, make the situation even worse. Luke assisted her up onto the seat of the buckboard.

Stanley Shields helped a wobbly Sammy to his feet and attempted to brush some of the dust off Sammy's suit.

"I guess," Sammy said, gasping for breath, "this means I won't be dancing at their wedding."

"Don't take Luke's poor humor to heart, son," Shields said to him. "If he really meant you harm, we wouldn't be talkin' now."

Shields escorted Sammy over to a bench next to the train station. "You best be toughin' up some if you want to survive in these parts," Shields said. "I'll give you this, boy: You got more guts that I would've thought, standin' up to Luke, or at least tryin' to. Lot of men would've stayed down the first time he flattened 'em. I seen Luke beat men even bigger'n his ownself."

"How about that," Sammy said weakly.

"You'll be all right, son," he said to Sammy. "Breathe deep, and try not to hold Luke's bad attitude against the Bar-S."

"You comin', Mr. Shields?" Luke asked, mounting his horse. Emily sat looking concerned. Billy and Elmer climbed onto their horses, thoroughly enjoying the festivities.

"I'm comin', I'm a-comin'," Shields yelled back. "Y'all still care to join us, Mr. Kaminsky?"

Sammy groaned and replied, "Thank you, Mr. Shields, but I think I'll live a lot longer if I stay here."

"Suit yourself," Shields said, and patted Sammy on the back. He left Sammy on the bench and walked back to his buckboard. He climbed aboard and snapped the reins, guiding the two-horse team around.

Luke and Emily's brothers trotted off with nary a glance at Sammy. As the wagon followed, kicking up dust, Emily turned in the seat and flashed Sammy a smile. He smiled back weakly as the wagon lurched away.

It wasn't until the wagon had vanished over the horizon that Sammy looked around. The depot was deserted, not a soul to be seen. There was a sign hanging from the telegraph office door that said, "Gone to dinner. Back in one hour."

Sammy had never felt so alone in his whole life.

Slocum lay flat on his back in the bed of the wagon, staring up at the beautiful sunset. Rose had loved sunsets. Slocum wished he had another bottle. He was halfway to sober, and that was halfway too far.

The buckboard was driven by a dark-skinned Comanche named Horace Sitting Duck. Sitting Duck did odd jobs around town, from shoveling horseapples at the stable to washing dishes at the restaurant to emptying spittoons at the saloons. This evening he was taking Slocum to the train station to pick up Rose's nephew from back east. Sitting Duck was covered with a dusty Indian blanket. A battered gray hat sat perched atop his greasy black hair, which was braided on either side of his wide face. Slocum was in no condition to do anything other than bounce around in the back of the wagon; it was as though Sitting Duck were going out of his way to hit every rock and gopher hole along the road.

Slocum sat up and said to Sitting Duck, "Over yonder is a rock you missed. Maybe you'd like to go back and run over it."

"All right," Sitting Duck said, "but it cost you extra."

Slocum said, "Can't you go any faster? Rose's nephew will be an old man by the time we get there."

"Old Comanche proverb say 'Rattlesnake that eat too many mice will move too slow to escape hungry eagle.' "

Slocum said, "And just what the hell is that supposed to mean?"

"Make more sense in Comanche," Sitting Duck said.

"Loses something in the translation at that," Slocum agreed. He lay down again and put his hat over his face to block out the last of the sun's rays. After days of sucking down hooch, he drifted off to sleep within seconds.

Slocum dreamed. He was chasing Rose all over town and into the hotel, where she disappeared up the stairs. In the dream, Slocum followed her up to the top floor. She vanished down another hallway. Slocum gave chase, his legs like rubber, and she turned to look back at him and smiled. She looked radiant and more beautiful than ever. She turned a corner. Slocum followed, and now she was as naked as a jaybird. She was waiting for him. He went to take her in his arms, and suddenly she turned into the widow Melody Daniels. She, too, was as naked as the day she was born.

Their lips were just about to touch in a passionate kiss when Sitting Duck jerked the horses' reins and brought the wagon to a lurching halt, slapping Slocum awake. He shook his head a few times to clear the alcoholic haze out of his head.

His vision cleared, but strangely he heard violin music. Slocum shook his head a couple more times, but the fiddle playing didn't go away. It wasn't square-dance fiddling though, more like a man would hear in an opera hall, if he was of a mind to go to an opera hall.

"Where are we?" Slocum asked grumpily.

"Train depot," Sitting Duck said.

"Is it just me, or do you hear a fiddle, too?" Slocum wanted to know.

Sitting Duck pointed toward the pasture north of the station. Under an old gnarly oak tree, someone was playing the fiddle, silhouetted in the setting sun.

"That be our man," Sitting Duck said.

Slocum scrambled out of the wagon and walked slowly toward the thin figure whose back was to him. The skinny dude appeared to be oblivious. He continued fiddling to the orange sunset.

Slocum stopped about ten feet away from the boy.

"Mighty fancy fiddlin', son," Slocum said.

Sammy turned around abruptly, his eyes wide. The cowboy standing before him seemed to loom eight feet tall, six feet of man and two feet of hat. He looked very much like Mr. Siringo, only taller. Much taller.

"If I disturbed the peace," Sammy said, the violin and bow held firmly in one hand at his side, "my apologies."

"Ain't no law against fiddlin', boy," Slocum said. "You wouldn't by chance be Rose's cousin Samuel from New York, would you?"

He nodded. "Are you Mr. Slocum?"

"John'll do fine," Slocum said. He extended his rough, calloused hand. Sammy took it and they shook. The kid had a grip softer than a featherbed.

Slocum looked Sammy up and down a couple of times. He was certainly dressed like a Yankee dude: suit, tie, derby, and black shoes that laced up to the ankle, fine for city living but as useless as a wild boar with teats for the harsh west Texas landscape. His clothes were caked with alkali dust and dirt. The kid had had a rough trip.

Upon closer examination, Slocum could see the kid was sporting the beginnings of a shiner, and his lip was split. There was blood on the lapels of his soiled white shirt.

"I see you've already had yourself a warm Texas welcome," Slocum said.

"I don't know what I did to make that man so angry," Sammy said.

"Don't take much in these parts," Slocum said. "We best be gettin' you back to town. Looks like you could use a bath and a change of clothes and a big steak."

"I am kind of hungry," Sammy said.

"I meant for that eye," Slocum said. "Though I guess we can rustle one up for your belly, too."

By this time, Sitting Duck had sauntered over to get a gander at Roseville's newest resident. Sammy had never seen an honest-to-God Indian savage in the flesh before. This one looked just like his wooden cousin who graced the entrance of Krepnik's Cigar Store on DeKalb Avenue.

Sammy cautiously took a few steps backward.

"Is he a real"—Sammy gulped—"Indian?"

"Half-breed." Slocum suppressed a smile. "Half Comanche, half rye whiskey," Slocum said.

Sitting Duck snorted. "Look who talking," he said. "Last three moons, Slocum become Chief Suck-It-Up."

"Just take his bag, please," Slocum said.

Sitting Duck grabbed the suitcase handle and hoisted the battered suitcase. The handle snapped off and the suitcase fell to the ground, popping open. It was empty.

"I heard of traveling light," Slocum said. "But this is goin' one extra."

"Somebody stole my clothes while I was asleep," Sammy explained sheepishly. "Somewhere outside Kansas City, I think."

Sitting Duck said, "Old Comanche proverb: 'Dung happen.'"

"Judging from those fancy-pants duds you're sportin'," Slocum said, "somebody did you a favor."

"I guess I'm not exactly dressed properly for this part of the world," Sammy said.

"We can fix that, too, I reckon," Slocum said. "We best be going."

Slocum and Sitting Duck started walking toward the wagon. Sammy stood dumbly, watching them. Slocum turned and shouted, "You comin' or not?"

Sammy started trotting after them, trying to put his violin and the bow in the case as he ran. About halfway there, Sammy's left foot got tangled in a root and he fell flat into the dirt, the violin case tumbling from his hands.

Slocum shook his head sadly. He said, "Can't say you're much like your cousin Rose."

Sammy spit out dirt. "So I've been told," he said.

8

Sammy had never tasted a chicken fried steak. He didn't know which half was the chicken and which half was the steak. It didn't matter.

He tore into it ravenously, his knife and fork working like a well-oiled machine. It was delicious, though probably a far piece from kosher. The fried potatoes were also tasty, though greasier than the axles of a peddler's wagon. Sammy ate them anyway.

Slocum sat opposite him at the cafe table, his ham and eggs sitting cold before him. His whiskey-soaked belly rebelled at the thought of solid food. He sipped tomato juice, more or less sober now. Binge drinking wasn't as easy these days as it had once been. Took longer to bounce back now, as evidenced by the sour burning in his belly. A huge whiskey headache was forming in his skull.

"You best slow down if you don't want your supper coming back up on you," Slocum said, watching Sammy shovel food into his mouth.

Sammy swallowed and nodded. "To be a glutton I didn't mean," he said. "It's just that I haven't eaten much these last few days."

Upon seeing the town of Roseville for the first time, Sammy had blurted out, "This is it?" and gone paler than fresh milk. Slocum guessed that the sight of the small, dusty Texas town had unnerved this city boy accustomed to the congested streets of New York.

Sammy had said nothing as Slocum pointed out each small building in town. "Blacksmith, livery, saloon, hotel, bank, saloon, telegraph, dress shop, saloon, bakery, whorehouse, and saloon," Slocum said. "They're all yours now, son, or pieces of 'em, anyway."

Sammy didn't seem to care, Slocum saw. He was in a state of shock, between the arduous journey and seeing the wild frontier town that was to be his new home. Sammy looked like he wanted either to cry or throw up, or maybe both.

Despite this, or maybe because of it, Sammy tore into his first real meal in days. Slocum figured the skinny kid needed sustenance before anything else. He'd need his strength to face what was to come, most of it anything but pleasant. Between Potter and the rest of the hungry buzzards around town swooping over Rose's holdings, things would get rough. This nervous, skinny kid from New York hardly looked up to the possibly deadly task that lay ahead.

"So where do we go from here?" Sammy asked.

"Thought we'd see about getting you some new duds at the mercantile. Then I figured on taking you over to Rose's house on the edge of town," Slocum said. "I reckon it's yours now. You can bathe and have yourself a shave, not that I see much that needs it."

"From no hair on my face I'm aware, thank you," Sammy responded. "From what I've seen from the men in this place, they should all be so lucky."

Slocum leaned back in his chair. "The Pinkertons tell you much about what to expect here?"

"A little," Sammy said, polishing off the last hunk of steak. He wiped a biscuit in the gravy. "He said my cousin's money was tied up in all sorts of businesses and things. He said there are some people who might get nasty about it. I thought to myself, Sammy, if anyone gives you trouble, go to the police station and tell them." He reached for another biscuit and added, "There *are* police in Roseville, aren't there?"

"Police?" Slocum said with a chuckle. "Son, the only law in this town is me. You're in Texas now, not Brooklyn, New York. We solve our own problems here, with talk if we can. With guns if we can't."

"You'll excuse me for asking, Mr. Slocum," Sammy said nervously, "but what kinds of problems were you thinking about?"

"Well—" Slocum started to say, then decided that the kid had enough to worry about for the time being. Let him get some rest first and then spring the bad news on him, when Sammy and his nerves were calmer. "Let's get you settled, then we'll study more on the subject. In the meantime," he said, "you look like you could use a nice slab of apple pie with a thick wedge of cheddar cheese."

Slocum yelled to the lady behind the counter, "A slice of apple pie for Miss Rose's cousin, Amelia."

"Coming up, Johnny," Amelia said. She was a sixtyish, gray-haired woman who reminded Sammy of his Aunt Meema.

"How well did you know my cousin Rose, Mr. Slocum?" Sammy asked.

"You could say we were close friends," Slocum said, looking a tad uncomfortable. He took the makings of a cigarette out of his shirt pocket and started rolling himself a smoke.

"I didn't mean to get personal," Sammy said. "I'm sorry to say that I never had the chance to meet her. I thought you could tell me what she was like. Was she nice? Was she pretty?"

"She was nice, she was pretty, and she was more," Slocum said, striking a match under the table and lighting his smoke. "How much do you know about her?"

"Just what my aunt and uncle told me," Sammy said. "Not very much. That she was rich."

"Did you know," Slocum said, "exactly *how* she got to be so rich?"

"That's the part that puzzles me," Sammy admitted. "We heard she went west and got rich. I think she did it by being sick."

"Come again?" Slocum said.

"Well, Uncle Jake said that cousin Rose made her money on her back."

"I guess you could say that," Slocum said. The kid would have to know the truth sooner or later. He said, "Son, your cousin started her fortune by running a high-class whorehouse in Colorado before she came to Texas."

"Whorehouse?" Sammy asked blankly.

"Yes," Slocum said. "You know what a whore is, don't you?"

"Sure," Sammy said, not sounding altogether sure. "It's what Aunt Meema calls the mayor of New York City."

"That's one kind," Slocum said. "But that ain't the one your cousin Rose built her fortune on."

"I'm not sure I understand," Sammy said, though he suspected some things.

"Whore," Slocum said. "Fallen women. They have it, men want it, they pay for it. Business and pleasure combined. The world's oldest profession."

Reality slowly dawned on Sammy. He recalled Esther Tannenbaum, the older girl who hung around the candy store and took some of the men in the neighborhood into a room in the back for ten or twenty minutes at a time. She dressed well and always had money, though she had no job that anyone could see. Sammy was warned to stay away from her. The Bible spoke of such things.

"My cousin Rose . . . was . . . like . . . Esther Tannenbaum?" Sammy said, choking.

"Never met Miss Tannenbaum," Slocum said, "but if she charged by the hour, the answer is yes."

Amelia placed a healthy slab of apple pie and cheese before Sammy, who ignored it. He took a long drink of water.

"I didn't know," Sammy said, barely above a hoarse whisper.

"Don't you be gettin' the wrong idea," Slocum said sharply. "Your cousin Rose was a fine woman, a straight-shooter and braver than any Texas Ranger. Honest, generous, too. She did what she had to do, son, to survive when times were hard.

"Besides," Slocum went on. "She also left you a fully staffed cathouse right here in town."

"She did?" Sammy asked, blinking rapidly.

"Six professional ladies, all at your beck and call," Slocum said. "Yours for the taking."

"Really?" Sammy asked, starting to squirm nervously.

"Let's get you some duds," Slocum said, standing, "and I'll take you over there. Got a nice, big bathtub and lots of hot water. Some friendly ladies, too."

Slocum gently took Sammy's arm and raised him out of his chair. "I don't suppose you'd mind being pampered by some pretty girls, would you?"

"Sammy Kaminsky is not a coward," Sammy said, "but neither is Sammy Kaminsky a *schmuck.*"

Sammy let Slocum guide him to the door, out into Roseville's muddy main street and toward a two-story house on the other side.

"You mean I . . . own this place?" Sammy stammered.

"Lock, stock, and pussy," Slocum said.

Sammy, his jaw dropping in wonderment, looked around the elegant parlor of the Roseville Happytime Emporium. Young, pretty, heavily made up women lounged in velvet-covered sofas, smiling shamelessly at him. Abraham Lincoln Botts was pounding away at the piano, a cigarette hanging from the corner of his mouth.

"John Slocum, as I live and breathe!" Esther Howard waddled toward them, dressed in an exquisite red dress that showed far too much of her sagging breasts. The relative dimness of the room and the makeup Esther applied by the shovelful managed to disguise some of her years, but not all.

She kissed Slocum on the mouth. It was like kissing a perfumed rattlesnake. Slocum pushed her away and forced a cordial smile.

"Meet your new boss, Esther," Slocum said. He took Sammy gently by the arm, and added, "Esther Howard, meet Samuel David Kaminsky."

Esther took Sammy's hand and gave it a squeeze, smiling from ear to ear, though Slocum saw no joy in her hard green eyes.

"He's so cute," Esther gushed, squeezing his left cheek. Sammy winced. "You look just like your cousin Rose," she added, and pulled a handkerchief from between her breasts. She dabbed at her eyes, becoming weepy. "Such a tragedy, cut down in her very prime of life. We'll all miss her terribly."

There was little conviction in her voice, even Sammy could tell.

"I guess you'll want to meet the staff," Esther went on, taking Sammy's arm and leading him to the women assembled all over the parlor. The first stop was a chunky redhead dressed in a pink corset and little else.

"This is Sharon, from Chicago," Esther said. "Sharon, say hello to Samuel."

"The pleasure is all mine," Sharon responded, sounding bored. She extended a limp hand. Sammy took it, and was reminded of a cold herring.

Esther escorted him away from Sharon and over to a busty brunette, bordering on pretty, though her looks were blunted by the hard life of her profession. She also had the largest breasts he'd ever seen. Sammy couldn't take his eyes off them.

"This is Amanda," Esther said. Amanda stood, and towered a good four inches over Sammy. He was a bit dismayed to see that she was barefoot.

"Pleased to make your acquaintance," Amanda said, and broke out in tears. "Oh, poor Miss Rose," she wailed, tears streaming from her eyes. "What will we do?"

She grabbed Sammy and gave him a smothering hug, blubbering helplessly, smashing his face between her twin moons. Breathing was a problem, but Sammy didn't mind.

Slocum pulled him away from her. "No point in killin' him his first day here, Amanda," he said.

Sammy was introduced to the other four employees of his late cousin's cathouse. There was Vivian, a slinky, sultry blonde who looked like she could devour Sammy in two bites; Mary Beth, a skinny, pasty-faced girl of no more than eighteen who Esther said came from a prominent Mississippi family but looked more like a sharecropper's daughter; then Evelyn, who stood all of five feet and weighed over two hundred pounds. She had curly brown hair and dimples deeper than a water well. She was busy greedily tearing chunks of meat off a chicken leg.

Sammy backed away. Esther said, "Evelyn is an acquired taste."

Sammy lost his appetite until Esther introduced him to the best looking of the bunch, a dusky, raven-haired girl about Sammy's age. She was almost the prettiest girl he'd ever seen, second only to the one on the train, Emily Shields. Sammy felt his heart flutter, and this time it wasn't a gas attack.

"Sammy, this is Louise," Esther said, seeing his unabashed interest. "I'm sure you two will find something to talk about."

"Hello, Sammy," Louise said in an accent he couldn't decipher, until Esther said, "Louise is a mixed breed. Half Cherokee, half white, and all passion."

Louise didn't look as hard as the others. Her smile was genuine, and her eyes still had the sparkle that seemed lost to her co-workers.

"It's a meeting to pleasure you," Sammy said nervously, his heart pounding. "I mean, it's a pleasure to eat you . . . uh, a pleasure to acquaint your makeance . . . make your meetance . . ." His mouth was dry. "Hello."

Esther said, "Mr. Kaminsky, do you have any questions?"

Sammy came back to reality, wresting his eyes from Louise's perfect figure and pixieish smile. He was suddenly aware of the piano music flowing melodiously behind him.

Sammy said, "Who's the gentleman playing the piano?"

"That's Abraham Lincoln Botts," Esther said, somewhat puzzled. "Why?"

"He plays wonderfully," Sammy said, his eyes transfixed by Abe's pudgy fingers as they expertly plinked the piano keys. Sammy made his way toward the piano. Abe stopped playing and gave Sammy a huge smile.

He extended his hand, the other still tickling the ivories.

Sammy took it and said, "That's a delightful melody you're playing, Mr. Botts. Does it have a name? I've never heard it before."

"Don't gots no name, as I recollect," Abe said. "Learned it back in New Orleans. I was thinkin' of callin' it the 'Miss Rose Song,' in her honor. One fine lady, yes indeedy."

Sammy, who had been clutching his violin all along, said, "Would you mind if I joined you?"

"Shore, join the party," Abe said, and took a swallow from the ever-present mug of beer he kept atop his piano.

Sammy removed the violin from the case and in no time was playing away with Abe in a rousing rendition of the "Miss Rose Song."

"You got pretty good rhythm for a white boy," Abe commented.

"Thank you," Sammy said, trying to keep up on the strings with Abe's driving beat. Professor Stossel would have been proud.

One by one, the girls gravitated to the two musicians, circling the piano and Sammy both, responding to the sweet music. They began to dance with one another, hooking elbows and two-stepping across the parlor floor.

Sammy, Slocum could see, was clearly having a good time. Only Louise sat while the others danced, her eyes never leaving Sammy.

"In all my years running cathouses, I've never seen such," Esther exclaimed. "Six willing women, and all he wants to do is play a fiddle."

Slocum, standing next to her, was busy rolling a cigarette. Somehow, he wasn't surprised that Sammy preferred playing his violin to dallying with the opposite sex. It seemed consistent with his behavior thus far.

Slocum said to Esther, "He needs a nice hot bath to get the prairie dust out of his pores. I trust you'll get the job done, Esther."

"He's in good hands with me, John," Esther said.

"That's what I'm afraid of," Slocum said. "I want to see him alive and smiling tomorrow morning. Keep your hands on his pecker and not around his throat."

"I get the impression you don't trust me, Mr. Slocum," Esther said.

"Rose always knew you were shortchanging her," Slocum said.

"Why didn't she fire me, then?" Esther said, sounding huffy.

"She was plannin' to," Slocum said. "Then the Fishers came and killed her. So I'm telling you this, Esther. I know you're smart, very smart. But don't get smart with me. I'll be keeping an eye on your books here, so don't even think about skimming the cream off this establishment."

"Your attitude shocks and dismays me, Mr. Slocum," Esther said, sounding hurt. Slocum wasn't having any.

"Not likely," Slocum said. "You run a good house, Esther, but Lord help you, you mess with Rose's kin, and I'll mess you ten times worse."

Esther turned to slap Slocum square in the face. He grabbed her wrist before she could.

"We'll see what Mr. Eustace Potter has to say about that," Esther said.

Slocum squeezed her wrist until she cried out. The girls stopped dancing to watch their madam, being subdued. The fat old witch had it coming. They were glad to see her get it.

"You picked the wrong side, Esther," Slocum said, clenching her wrist. "But there's still time to see the evil of your ways."

"Potter's going to kill you, Slocum," Esther hissed.

Slocum gave her arm a firm, painful twist. She howled. Sammy stopped playing and watched with some alarm.

"Mr. Slocum," Sammy said. "If it's not too much trouble, would you mind letting this poor woman—"

"You shut your mouth, boy," Slocum snapped. He held Esther firmly. "And don't open it until you know the way things work in this town. I'll handle this situation, unless you have any objections. Your cousin Rose entrusted me to make sure you got everything that's coming to you, and by God I promised to do just that. But don't try my patience, Sammy, 'cause it's wearing mighty thin just about now."

Sammy's lips twitched a few times, but no sounds came out. "I'm sorry . . . ," he stuttered. "I didn't mean . . ."

"This business belongs to you, walnuthead," Slocum snapped. "This woman will steal the second hand off a clock if you turn a blind eye to her. Remember that."

Slocum stomped over to the front door and flung it open. He said to Esther, who was rubbing her sore wrist, "Like I said, the man needs a bath. See that he gets one, and in the style befitting his stature in this town."

Sammy stared at Slocum, blinking rapidly.

"I'm going out to get you some new duds, son," Slocum said. "Get some rest, if these ladies let you. We got us a busy day tomorrow."

Slocum went out, slamming the door behind him. Abe started tickling the piano keys again, whipping into a hot rendition of "Good Night Ladies."

Esther, scowling, spit on the floor and turned to her whores.

"Who wants to give Mr. Kaminsky a bath?" she asked. Louise shot Sammy a smile.

"I'll be happy to do it, Miss Esther," she said.

Sammy, without realizing it, started smiling. Louise rose from a velvet chair and walked over to him. She took the violin and the bow from his hands and placed them gently into the case, then took his hand and led him to the staircase. Sammy had no choice but to follow.

"Treat him right, Louise," Esther said, "or there'll be hell to pay."

"We'll be fine, ma'am," Louise said. She climbed the stairs seductively, beckoning Sammy to follow.

Sammy swallowed hard, watching Louise's slim, shapely behind ascend the stairs. Halfway up, she turned back to him and said huskily, "Coming, Mr. Kaminsky?"

Sammy felt a cold sweat break out across his forehead and in his armpits. He looked at Abe desperately, as if for some kind of guidance.

"Was I you," Abe said to him, "I'd get my little ass up there right now."

"Perhaps I should," Sammy said nervously. He started climbing the stairs after Louise, venturing into waters heretofore uncharted.

9

Slocum grabbed a couple of pairs of blue jeans and carried them up to the register at the Roseville Mercantile. Hiram Quick took them from Slocum and put them down on the counter, next to the pair of calfskin boots he'd picked out for Sammy.

"Hope them britches ain't for y'all," Quick said. "Look a trifle small, John."

"They ain't for me; they're for a skinny kid from back east," Slocum said.

"Of course," Quick said. "Miss Rose's kin from New York. Heared he was a-comin' to town."

"He's here," Slocum said, "and the clothes he's wearing now'll get him killed for sure. Best give me some shirts, too, Hiram, and some underwear."

Quick nodded and went back into the storeroom for the goods.

"What size?" Quick asked.

"The smaller the better."

The bell above the door tinkled, and in walked the always lovely widow Melody Daniels. Her face lit up like a prairie fire when she saw Slocum. She was dressed in a frilly white dress and matching bonnet.

"Good evening, Mr. Slocum," she said with a smile.

Slocum took off his hat and said, "How do, ma'am." My, but she did look fetching, and he'd fetched nothing since Rose's untimely death.

"Buying a new wardrobe, Mr. Slocum?" she asked.

"These ain't for me," Slocum said. "They're for Rose's cousin from back east."

"Oh, yes. Mr. Kaminsky," Melody said. "I heard about him. Where is he?"

"Over to the whore—Uh, he's cleaning up over yonder," Slocum stammered.

Quick came toddling in from the back room carrying some boxes. He greeted Miss Melody warmly. "What can I do for you, Miss Melody?"

"I need some molasses, a sack of flower, and some saltine crackers," she said. Then, as an afterthought, she added, "And some apples, about a dozen, and six cans of peaches."

Quick grinned and started pulling the items from the shelves behind him. He said, "Should I have it delivered, Miss Melody? Seems a trifle much for one body to carry."

Melody turned to Slocum and placed her hand on his arm. "Perhaps Mr. Slocum would be kind enough to help me."

"Well, I . . . I'm not sure—" Slocum started to protest, for no good reason he could think of. Miss Melody was extremely desirable, but he still missed Rose.

On the other hand, he knew, it was time to get on with his life, sooner or later. Noticing the tantalizing swell of her breasts, Slocum decided it would be sooner. Samuel Kaminsky was safely tucked away at the whorehouse and would be occupied for the time being.

"I've got a nice stew simmering on the stove," Miss Melody said as Quick finished packing up her goods. "I'd be honored if you would join my daughter and myself for dinner, Mr. Slocum."

She smiled demurely, but Slocum could see fire in her eyes. Quick was nodding approvingly. Slocum had the feeling he was being set up for something.

"I do believe that would be very nice, Miss Melody," he said, curling an arm around the wooden crate of groceries. He hoisted the crate and said, "After you, ma'am."

Melody said, "Please put this on my account, Mr. Quick."

"Yes'm," he said. Melody turned and walked out, swinging her hips. Both Slocum and Quick stared at her shapely behind as she went through the door.

As the bell tinkled, she said, "Coming, Mr. Slocum?" Slocum snapped out of his trance. Miss Melody said, "That is if you're done staring at my derriere."

Slocum, turning red in the face, followed her out the door.

"It's okay, you can take your clothes off in front of me," Louise said. "I'm used to it."

Sammy had never undressed in front of any woman, unless one included when he was a child and Aunt Meema helped him get ready for bed. Unlike any of his friends, Sammy had never even played "you show me yours and I'll show you mine" with any of the neighborhood girls, a game also known as Find the Salami. Now here he was, standing before a filled porcelain bathtub, with a pretty woman expecting him to drop his drawers.

"If you want to take a bath before this water gets cold," Louise said, "you best shed your britches and climb on in."

Sammy sat on the edge of the bed. He took off his shoes, then started to unbutton his shirt. He got half-way down and said sheepishly, "Would you mind turning around, please?"

"I think you're shy," Louise said with a chuckle.

"I think I'm shy, too," Sammy said.

"Would it be any easier if I undress first?" Louise asked.

"It couldn't hurt," Sammy said. Louise started to disrobe, peeling off her undergarments. Sammy, to be courteous, covered his eyes.

Louise said, "It's okay if you want to watch. Some men think that's half the fun."

Sammy peeked through his fingers. Louise smiled and stripped down to her bare essentials. Sammy's mouth dropped open as he gazed hungrily at Louise's firm, upturned breasts and hourglass figure. Granted, there was maybe a little too much sand on the bottom of that hourglass, but the important thing was, this woman was indeed naked. Naked women had been only a wild fantasy for Samuel David Kaminsky. The closest he'd been to one was walking in on Aunt Meema accidentally as she was getting dressed, which Sammy didn't count. There was also that time when Sammy had barged in on Monk Westman after being summoned for another command violin performance. Monk had been fondling the breasts of his ugly girlfriend when Sammy entered his headquarters. Sammy had been mortified. He was turning to leave when Monk said to him, "Stick around, kid. Play good and maybe I'll give you a taste."

Sammy, clutching his violin, had bolted out the door to the sound of Monk's laughter. He had run back home, locked himself in the outhouse in the courtyard, and played the "Minute Waltz" in forty seconds, snapping two strings in the process.

And now here was an attractive woman standing naked before him, willing and ready, waiting for Sammy to make the next move.

"Your turn," Louise said, going to him and unbuttoning the last two buttons on his shirt. That done, she peeled the shirt off, then started unbuckling his pants.

Sweating like a pig, Sammy said, "I could play you something on my violin. Do you like Beethoven?"

Louise dropped to her knees and started yanking Sammy's pants down.

He sweated harder and stammered, "Mozart. I'll play Mozart. Do you like Mozart's Movement in Number Seven?"

"Only movements I like are the kind I do every mornin'," Louise said. When his pants were down around his ankles, she said, "Now, just shut your piehole and step out of these britches." That Sammy's member had swollen to the size of a ripe cucumber and was standing proudly at attention was not lost on a seasoned professional like Louise.

Sammy did as he was told.

Louise didn't give him time to be embarrassed. She grabbed his stiff manhood and guided him over to the bathtub, then pushed him ass-backward into the hot water.

"You got a week's worth of dirt on you, boy," Louise said. "I ain't in no mood to be covered in it. Be time for that when I'm dead."

She grabbed a pail, scooped out some hot water and dumped it over Sammy's head. With one hand she grabbed a bar of soap from off a dish on the edge of the tub, and with the other she again took hold of Sammy's manhood to soap up his genitals, her breasts rubbing against Sammy's cheeks. With no warning, everything below Sammy's waist seemed to erupt, and a stream of jism shot from the hot wells within him.

Louise couldn't have cared less. One in the hand was worth three in the bush, she knew. She continued to scrub him down, sliding the soap up and down Sammy's bare, scrawny chest.

Sammy hung his head in shame at having shot his seed in Louise's presence. Louise saw his discomfort and said, "Don't worry, boy. You'll be comin' around that mountain again before you know it."

"If you'll be so kind, Mr. Slocum," Melody Daniels said, "to pull the loaf from my oven."

"Ma'am?" Slocum asked, gazing at Melody's breasts, which were straining against the confines of her dress, the nipples rearing their lovely heads.

"The bread," Melody said, pointing to the oven with a knife, which she'd been using to slice tomatoes. "I think it's ready."

Slocum's mind snapped back to the real world. He leapt from the kitchen chair, grabbed the red-hot oven handle with his bare hand, and pulled it open. He had started to pull the freshly baked loaf of bread from the rack when the pain shot up his arms.

Slocum howled in agony, clutching his burned fingers. Melody dropped the knife and came rushing over to him. She gently took his hand and examined it. "Not too serious," she said. "It seems your mind is elsewhere, Mr. Slocum."

"I reckon it is," he said, as she dabbed over his singed fingers fresh butter from a dish on the table. They gazed into each other's eyes. Slocum's pain was suddenly forgotten. He started to drown in her sea-green eyes, not minding a bit.

"You miss her, don't you?" Melody asked tenderly. Her concern was genuine.

Actually, Slocum had been trying his damndest to put Rose out of his mind while in the presence of the most attractive Melody Daniels.

He said, "Reckon I do." He hung his head, looking grim. Melody took Slocum's hand to her bosom and pressed it flat against her. Slocum's heart lurched. Was it too soon after Rose had been laid to rest, he asked himself, to be attracted to anyone? It was a decision unlike any other he'd been forced to make in his life, and not one that could be taken lightly. Still, his hand *was* planted firmly on her boob. Slocum felt as if his conscience and his manhood were locked in mortal combat.

Melody embraced him and held him tightly against her. "Let me share your pain, John," she whispered in his ear. "Just tell me . . . how can I help you?"

"I can think of a million things," Slocum whispered back. So much for letting his conscience be his guide.

Miss Melody gave him a hard, passionate kiss. Slocum couldn't help but reciprocate. This was a very thoughtful woman.

After a few moments, she took his hand and maneuvered him toward the bedroom.

Slocum dimly recalled the old saying about climbing back onto an unbroke mare after getting thrown, and let himself be led. He also remembered, suddenly, that Miss Melody had a baby daughter.

"Your daughter," Slocum started to say. "Is she—"

"Fast asleep," Melody whispered in his ear. "In the back room. She's a very sound sleeper."

She ushered Slocum into the bedroom and closed the door behind them. She unbuckled his gunbelt, and it dropped to the floor.

"I just want you to know, Mr. Slocum," she said, backing away from him toward the bed, "that I think you're a very nice man, and I don't like to see a nice man such as yourself in pain."

"Funny, neither do I," Slocum said.

Melody turned her back to him and said, "Would you mind unbuttoning me, Mr. Slocum?"

"I think that would make me feel much better, Miss Melody," he said.

He did as she'd asked. Underneath was a very well-proportioned young woman held captive in a starched petticoat. Slocum breathed deeply and smelled, along with her fragrant perfume, the aroma of burning bread.

"I think your bread is burning," Slocum said, unbuttoning his shirt slowly.

"Let it," Melody said. She eased him down onto the bed and crawled seductively on top of him.

Louise scrubbed Sammy's chest with a washcloth, her bare breasts quivering enticingly a mere inch before his eyes, like pendulums, hypnotizing him.

"You—you have lovely . . . uh . . . um . . . brea— uh . . . I mean—" Sammy tried to form the words, but they refused to come.

"Titties," Louise said, the washcloth plunging down to his crotch. "The word out here is titties. Don't know what you call 'em back east."

"I never called them anything," Sammy said. "I only stared at them."

"I figured as much," Louise said. Sammy only wanted to take her plump, red nipples between his lips and suck them until they were harder than a month-old bagel. "How long you been a virgin?"

"I'm not a virgin," Sammy said. "I'm Jewish."

"One don't have nothin' to do with the other, honey," Louise said. "I got a hunch you were out of town the day they talked about the birds and bees."

"No . . . I was there," Sammy said. "Birds I know. I mean, I've seen pigeons in the park. But I've never seen a bee."

"How would you like to get stung?" Louise asked, shoving her breasts even closer to his face.

She grabbed Sammy's swollen member and started caressing it. Until now, the only hand that had touched his *schlong* had been his own. It felt especially nice when the hand belonged to a pretty woman.

"I'd say you're as clean as a man can be," Louise said. "Would you like to go to the bed now?"

"You mean . . . like you and me and us?" Sammy asked. He tried to swallow, but his throat was dry.

Louise padded over to the bed and climbed between the cool sheets. She lay flat on the her back and spread her legs far apart. Her breasts poked invitingly up under the sheets, two miniature mountains Sammy wanted to scale at once. "Trust me, Sammy," she said. "It ain't gonna hurt one little bit."

"My Aunt Meema told me I could get blind doing nasty things with a woman I wasn't married to," Sammy said.

"Your auntie ain't here now, is she?" Louise said, rolling the top sheet on the bed down just above her nipples. "Ten minutes with me, and you'll see things in a whole different light."

Sammy's member rose to the occasion again, creating ripples in the bathwater. He gazed hungrily at the willing woman lying in the bed. Consumed by curiosity and lust, he stepped out of the bathtub, sudsy water dripping from his body. Sammy felt a raw hunger burning out of control within him.

He walked slowly to the bed, where Louise was beckoning him with outstretched arms. Sammy went to her, a man with a mission, and got his foot tangled in some frayed carpet strings. Flailing his arms uselessly, Sammy tripped over himself and crashed face-first onto the floor.

He looked up at Louise with an embarrassed grin. "Sorry."

"We got all night, lover," Louise said. "But you best get over here before you kill yourself."

Sammy got clumsily to his feet and felt himself being drawn to the woman lying in the bed. He climbed under the sheets and reached for her. She came into his arms and kissed him on the mouth. She wrapped her long legs around him, engulfing him. She gently grabbed his pulsing member and attempted to guide him into her. Before she could, though, Sammy's anticipation got the better of him—or the worst, he would muse later—and he erupted again, shooting his sticky seed into her fist.

"*Oy*," Sammy groaned. "*Oy vey esmere!*"

"If lovemaking was a gunfight, you'd be Johnny Ringo," Louise said, taking Sammy's enthusiasm totally in stride. "Don't worry about it, sugar," she added, wiping her hand on a towel. "Happens to the best of them. And we got *all* night to get it right."

"We do?" Sammy asked incredulously. He remembered a lot of his friends back in Brooklyn, the braver ones, complaining about the severe time limits on the girls at Cockeyed Sadie's, a whorehouse on Delancey Street, on Manhattan's Lower East Side. Many fathers from Williamsburg's Jewish community took their sixteen- or seventeen-year old sons to Cockeyed Sadie's as a rite of passage; also, it was safer in the long run than having a lot of pregnant, unwed girls running amok.

"Sure," Louise said. "You forgot that you own this place now. And as far as I'm concerned, honey, as long as you're the boss, you can come any old time you're of a mind to."

"So *long,*" Melody groaned as Slocum thrust his hips, sliding in and out of her like a hot knife through creamy butter. "So long!"

"So I've been told," Slocum gasped, sliding his hands under her firm, bare buttocks and clenching them. Melody brought her knees up and wrapped herself around Slocum, taking him inside her even more deeply.

"It's been so *long,*" Melody said, digging her sharp nails into Slocum's back and nibbling on his ear as he pumped away. In the kitchen, smoke from the burning bread seeped out of the oven. "You're like a cool rain in July."

"The drought is over, Missy," Slocum said.

"Oh, John," Melody responded breathlessly as their sweaty bodies intertwined passionately and made sweet music together. She kissed his lips hungrily. She said, "Let me help you, John. Let me help you forget!"

Slocum appreciated her concern, but he wasn't likely to forget this night, or Melody Daniels.

He continued pumping her until he felt the familiar, pleasant tingle in his groin. Paradise was but seconds away.

"Lord, I do love women," Slocum said. " 'Specially when they're under me."

"Men got their uses, too." Melody shuddered in ecstasy.

They climaxed together. The bread continued to burn, filling the whole house with smoke.

For the rest of his days, John Slocum would associate the aroma of burning bread with passionate lovemaking. And the mere sight of toast would hereafter get a pleasant rise out of him.

"He's up there in the whorehouse," Eustace Potter said, and took a swig of whiskey. "I want him dead."

They were sitting around a table in the Pink Garter saloon, sharing a bottle: Potter; his foreman and willing associate in crime, Al Bridge; and two of Potter's most trusted hands, Wilson Gregory and a half-Apache, half-Chinese plug-ugly called Flat Eye. The story went that Flat Eye's mother, the mail-order bride of an Oriental chef in New Orleans, was kidnapped by Apaches en route to marry her husband. Flat Eye's father was the feared war chief Galloping Ghost, who had led the murder raid on the wagon bringing Flat Eye's mother east. Galloping Ghost and his braves slaughtered everyone in the wagon except for the black-haired, slant-eyed Oriental woman, the yellow likes of which Galloping Ghost had never seen.

Al Bridge, who'd been doing Potter's evil bidding since they were wild and wooly drovers together in Oklahoma Territory years back, was a tall, thin man with beady black eyes and a tiny mustache that looked like a cockroach had fallen asleep on his upper lip. For twenty years he'd been helping his old saddlemate crush and destroy the competition, driving out sodbusters and sheep farmers in the territory.

Wilson J. Gregory III was a Harvard-educated man of twenty-two from an upper-crust Baltimore shipping family. Debutante balls and snot-nosed society parties bored him, so at age seventeen, Wilson J. Gregory III had cracked his father's head open with a poker and rifled the family safe of over fifty thousand dollars in cash. He headed west, where his natural inclination toward violence and bloodshed came in handy during range wars and assorted mayhem. Potter, recognizing good talent, eagerly employed him.

"Where's Slocum?" Potter wanted to know.

Nobody wanted to answer this one, for Potter, whose anemic, tired wife had died two years earlier, had been actively courting Melody Daniels. She wanted nothing to do with the foul-smelling, unshaven, but rich, rancher. That Slocum was probably doing to her what Potter could only dream of doing was not something any of them wanted to discuss with their violent boss.

"Well?" Potter snapped, slamming his fist onto the table. The bottle and glasses bounced up an inch. "I'm payin' you fatheads to keep an eye on the bastard. Where the hell is he?"

Flat Eye and Gregory looked to Al Bridge. He had known Potter the longest and were used to, but still afraid of, the boss's mean streak.

"He's duly occupied, Eustace," Bridge said, skipping over details. "He won't bother us. Tucked away for the night."

"Where?" Potter asked suspiciously, downing the rest of the whiskey from his glass.

"Well—" Bridge started. Lying to Potter was bad, but now the truth could hurt worse. He poured some whiskey into his glass and downed it in one gulp. He closed his eyes, gritted his teeth, and said, "He's with the widow Melody Daniels."

Bridge kept his eyes shut, waiting for the blast of Potter's gun and the pain of the bullet entering his brain. Neither came. Bridge cautiously opened one eye.

The truth of the situation was having no trouble dawning on Potter, whose face was turning a dark shade of red, the thick vein in his neck bulging hideously. He squeezed the shot glass until it cracked into three pieces and blood oozed from his huge fist.

Bridge knew that his old friend Potter never let his pecker get in the way of a wise business decision, but he could tell that this one was coming damn close. Potter finished grinding his teeth in anger. He took a long swig from the bottle. The crisis was over. For now.

"I want that little Yankee peckerwood to run so far away it'll cost him fifty dollars to send a letter," Potter said, anger seething from every pore. He took another big swig, then wiped his mouth on his sleeve. "You're sure he's still at the whorehouse?"

"If he came out, I would have heard," Gregory said.

"Then let's go talk to him," Potter said, standing abruptly, knocking his chair backward onto the floor. "Persuade his skinny hide that hangin' around Roseville ain't beneficial to his well-bein'."

The others stood as well. Flat Eye said, "Confucius say, 'Let wit be your sword, and bravery your armor.'" He frowned, thinking. "Or was it Geronimo?"

"Blow it out your ass," Bridge said.

"Go, brother, go," Abraham Lincoln Botts said, pounding his piano in the whorehouse parlor. Next to him, Sammy plucked some sweet chords from his fiddle. Together they played a rousing rendition of "Waltz Me Again, Tillie." To Sammy's amazement, Abe was familiar with the melody; he explained that it was nothing but an old Negro spiritual. Still, Sammy was impressed. And he was the only white man Abe had ever met who played as fast as he did.

Sammy's third attempt at lovemaking had succeeded, sort of. Or so he hoped; he wasn't sure. It was Sammy's understanding that a man had actually to "shoot a wad" inside the woman. Sammy wasn't quite certain he'd gone that far. He'd been in sort of a daze. What's more, he kept seeing the face of the girl he'd met on the train, Emily Shields, in his mind whenever he coupled with Louise. Louise was the best tutor money could buy. Not that he'd needed any—he owned a whorehouse.

Today Sammy was a man, sort of. Officially, his manhood had come with his *bar mitzvah* at the age of thirteen, but that was a religious ceremony that had nothing to do with sex. Sammy decided that there was a Jewish brand of manhood, and another that came with "cashing in your cherry," as Louise had put it.

Whatever. Sammy felt like a million dollars. After taking his virginity, or something along that line, Louise had served him an early breakfast in bed, buttering his toast and feeding him bacon and eggs. Sammy had devoured three strips of the greasy but delicious pork before asking what it was. He wasn't too upset with the answer.

"Look at it this way," Louise said. "You're a man what owns a whorehouse, a saloon, and a bank, and then some. That's every man's fantasy come true, and you can live it if you've a mind to."

Sammy decided to try.

Some of the cathouse girls were all clustered around the piano while others danced with one another. Even Esther Howard sat on the sofa, tapping her foot in time to the music.

"Where's a white boy such as yourself get that rhythm?" Abe asked, tickling the piano keys.

"I don't know," Sammy said. "Maybe my ancestors were from the Black Sea."

At the height of the revelry, they heard a loud crash in the hallway and the sounds of glass breaking. Esther jumped up from the couch. Eustace Potter, roaring drunk, came charging into the parlor like a furious, snot-snorting bull. Behind him were Al Bridge, Flat Eye, and Wilson Gregory III.

"Where is he?" Potter bellowed, swallowing the last of the whiskey. He flung the empty bottle across the room, where it exploded against the wallpaper. "Where's that damn Yankee boy?"

"Eustace," Esther cried, taking his arm. "Don't—"

Potter backhanded her solidly across the left side of her face and sent her sprawling onto the couch. He turned and grabbed one of the girls, Mary Beth, by her long, black hair. His men watched impassively. He yanked her head back and snarled, breathing whiskey fumes in her face, "I ast a question! And I best get me a answer."

Mary Beth whimpered in pain as Potter gave her hair another healthy yank. Sammy felt weak in the knees as he watched this enormous, terrifying man. His knees started knocking when it dawned on him that he himself was the damn Yankee boy Potter was not-so-gently inquiring about.

Al Bridge piped up. "That's him, Boss, with the fiddle."

Potter turned and cast a murderous glare at Sammy.

Sammy's bowels turned into ice water. He couldn't help but notice the very big gun holstered on Potter's huge hip.

Potter growled deep in his throat, like a wild boar in a cabbage patch. Sammy saw crooked teeth blackened by years of tobacco chewing.

"You little pissant," Potter hissed, grinning drunkenly. "You're a dead man."

Sammy instinctively shrank away from Potter's towering form as the enraged rancher took his first steps toward him.

"Was I playing off-key?" was all Sammy could think to say as Potter's looming shadow engulfed him.

10

It was even better the fourth time.

He and Melody were making passionate love. Slocum was on top of her, and they were doing it slow and sweet this time around. Slocum loved the feel of her erect nipples against his chest.

Melody suddenly stopped writhing under him, and Slocum felt her tense. She gasped.

"I do believe, Mr. Slocum," she whispered in his ear, "that there appears to be a large Indian standing at the foot of the bed."

Slocum craned his neck around, still atop her, "Sitting Duck," he said sharply. "Jumping butterballs, what the hell are you doing here?"

"Man like water buffalo stampeding into land of pleasure," Sitting Duck said, shrouded in darkness.

"Talk American, will you?" Slocum said. Melody squirmed out from under him and pulled the sheets up to her chin.

"If you don't mind," she said indignantly. She'd seen Sitting Duck around town, but never in her bedroom. Especially when she was buck naked.

"Your friend from back east in deep, dark trouble," Sitting Duck said. "Potter go into whorehouse with other men. Bridge, Gregory, and half-breed with funny eyes. All got bellyful hooch. Potter say he kill Yankee boy."

"Shit," Slocum sputtered, leaping from the bed and grabbing his pants. He hopped around on one foot and succeeded in putting his pants on backward. Sitting Duck followed him around the room, holding out his shirt as Slocum bounced around on the floor like a wounded rabbit.

Slocum flopped down on the edge of the bed and yanked off the backward pants. Sitting Duck gently put Slocum's hat onto his head. Slocum cursed and flung the hat onto the bed impatiently, trying to get his pants on properly. Sitting Duck patiently put the hat back onto Slocum's head. Slocum flung the hat off again and started straightening out his balled-up socks. Sitting Duck, never changing his expression, placed the hat on Slocum's head a third time, and for the third time Slocum ripped it off and slammed it on the bed beside him.

"Would you stop with the damned hat," Slocum snapped at the Indian.

Sitting Duck said impassively, "Sorry. Nervous energy."

Slocum finished dressing and yanked on his boots. He turned to Melody, who was still clutching the sheet, and said, "I'm sorry about this, Melody. Should never have left him alone."

Melody said, "He's a big boy, John. I'm sure he can handle himself."

"No!" Sammy cried in anguish as Eustace Potter snatched the violin from his hand and smashed it into splinters on top of the piano.

Abraham Lincoln Botts had been sitting motionless on his piano stool up to this point. To do otherwise would be suicidal. It was no secret that Eustace Potter liked to hurt folks.

Nonetheless, when he heard the crunch of wood on wood and saw the shattered remains of Sammy's violin, accompanied by the guffaws of Potter's goons, his blood boiled. He leapt to his feet before he could think the better of it, and opened his mouth to curse Potter.

A shot rang out before Abe could utter a syllable, and the black bowler hat flew off his head.

"Sit down, boy," Bridge said, holstering his pistol. "Next one might be closer to home."

Abe obediently sat back down.

Potter flung the remains of the violin aside and grabbed Sammy by the lapels. He lifted him a good fifteen inches off the floor so that they were eye to eye.

"I hate you," Potter seethed between clenched, black teeth.

"Maybe if you got to know me a little better—" Sammy stammered.

Too late, Sammy knew that Potter was beyond any form of reason. He felt himself being propelled backward from the force of Potter's thrust. Sammy was vaguely aware that he was actually airborne, flailing his arms uselessly. He plummeted into a crushed red velvet chair and tumbled ass-backward, feet over shoulders, giving him a view of his knees he'd never had before.

Sammy tried to move, but it proved impossible. His head and shoulders were propped up against the wall, his legs dangling over the upturned chair.

Potter loomed hugely above him. Sammy saw the barrel of a gun in Potter's hand as it came down, and he felt cold metal between his eyes.

"I want you out of town," Potter said. "Tonight. In one hour. If I see your scrawny Yankee butt on the street tomorrow, so help me Jesus I'll rip your head off and feed it to my pigs. You understand me, boy?"

Sammy knew he was being called upon to respond, but the act of speech refused to come.

Slocum crept undetected into the whorehouse and slipped up silently behind Gregory, who was drunk and off his guard. Slocum stuck the barrel of his gun into the small of Gregory's back and skillfully eased the pistol out of his holster.

"One word and you're dead," Slocum hissed.

Potter, meanwhile, was still poised over Sammy, the gun still dangerously close to Sammy's face.

"I ast you a question, boy!" Potter bellowed. "Answer me or I'll—"

"Fun's over, Potter," Slocum barked. "Drop it."

Potter froze at the sound of Slocum's voice. At the same time, Flat Eye, standing about eight feet from Slocum and Bridge, decided to get ambitious. He reached for his six-shooter.

Like lightning, Slocum pushed Gregory away, pivoted to the left, and fired three slugs into Flat Eye's chest. Flat Eye was dead before he hit the ground. Esther Howard and the rest of the whores started diving for cover.

Potter was about to fire on Slocum when another shot rang out and a chunk of wallpaper and plaster exploded directly behind Potter, an inch above his head. Sitting Duck, aiming a shotgun, stood behind Slocum, discouraging any further trouble. Bridge didn't have time to draw his weapon, and wisely decided not even to try.

"I said drop it," Slocum repeated.

Potter dropped his gun. It bounced off Sammy's noggin.

"I think it would be in your best interest to head on home, Potter," Slocum said, and motioned to Flat Eye's lifeless carcass. "And take your trash with you."

Bridge and Gregory remained motionless until Slocum snapped, "You heard me. Get a move on."

Bridge looked at Potter for some sort of confirmation. Potter nodded. Bridge and Gregory lifted Flat Eye and carried him outside.

"Now you get the hell out of here," Slocum said to Potter, "and leave the boy alone."

Potter, no less humble for the experience, made his way toward the door. He stopped and said to Slocum, "You just made the biggest mistake of your miserable life, Slocum.

So help me, I'll see your name on a tombstone pretty soon."

"If I thought you could read, maybe I'd be worried," Slocum said. "But I doubt it."

Potter exited, cursing a blue streak.

Slocum walked over to Sammy's inert form and said, "You all right, son?"

"To tell the honest truth," Sammy said, still sprawled against the wall, "I've been better."

11

"I appreciate everything you've tried to do, Mr. Slocum," Sammy said. "I really do. But I don't get the feeling I'm appreciated in this *shtetl*—excuse me, this village."

They were at Rose's house, where Sammy was tossing the few articles of clothing he had into a burlap sack. Sitting Duck was on the sofa carefully folding Sammy's sole pair of pants.

"Running from trouble ain't going to solve anything," Slocum said from the kitchen, pouring coffee into a cup. He added a strong dollop of the whiskey Rose had kept behind a tin of sugar. For snakebite, of course.

"You'll forgive me, but *not* running away will solve a lot less," Sammy said. He still had the shakes. The memories of Potter smashing his violin and Flat Eye's blood splattering all over the parlor were still vividly fresh in Sammy's mind.

"Here," Slocum said, handing Sammy the cup. "Drink this. It's good for your nerves."

Sammy reached for the cup with trembling hands and took a big swig. He coughed violently.

"What's in here, *schnapps*?" he sputtered.

"We call it whiskey out west," Slocum said.

"That's very good," Sammy said, handing Slocum the

cup. "But I'm going home, where whiskey is *schnapps* and people don't throw you across rooms or smash your violin or put guns in your face."

"Sammy," Slocum said, "he's just trying to scare you into running away so he and the rest of the greedy sidewinders in this town can grab everything. If you ain't here to stop 'em, they'll do just that."

"With all due respect, Mr. Slocum, my life is worth more than this *meshuga* Roseland."

"Roseville," Slocum corrected.

"Roseville, shmoesville," Sammy said. "I'm going back to New York."

"Frankly," Slocum said, "I can't believe you're scared of a fat old pisspot like Eustace Potter."

"You want to know how much I'm scared?" Sammy asked. He pointed to his scalp. "From here, right down to my socks."

Sitting Duck grunted. "Old Comanche saying: Hero die one hundred time, coward only once."

"It's the other way around," Slocum said.

"That's once too many," Sammy said.

"Let me ask you this," Slocum said. "How'd you plan on gettin' to the train station? It's fifteen miles as the buzzard flies."

"So I'll walk."

"And what were you plannin' on using for money?" Slocum said.

Slocum had him there. Sammy had a total of nine cents in his pocket. He said, "If you'd be so kind as to lend me enough for me to get home and maybe something for a little *nosh,* I'd be grateful. You have my promise I'll have my uncle send you the money as soon as I get home."

Slocum shook his head. "Can't do it, son. Conscience wouldn't let me. I promised you I'd do my best to back you up, but that don't include helping you run away."

"I have an excellent idea," Sammy said. "You can have half of everything, just send my half home to New York. Twenty-two Knickerbocker Avenue, Brooklyn, America."

"Don't think so, Sam," Slocum said. "Soon as I see you get what's yours, I'll be on my way. I never reckoned on putting down roots here. What I *will* do is teach you how to defend yourself so's you can stand up to Potter and the rest and lay claim to your fortune."

"Fortune, shmortune," Sammy snapped. "You can't spend a fortune when you're laying in a box with six feet of *schmootz* on top of you."

"So, fine," Slocum said irritably. He'd been pulled out of a sweet woman's bed and killed a man, and now he was arguing with this cowardly little shit. "So go, get the hell out. Go back east to your apron strings. Find a nice, warm bed to hide under. Let everyone in Williamsburg know what a gutless little gopher you are."

He grabbed Sammy's nose between his thumb and fore-finger and gave it a painful twist. Sammy howled in pain.

"That hurts!" Sammy cried.

"Listen to me, you scurvy little caterpillar," Slocum hissed. "You're stayin' here and no mistake."

"They don't like me," Sammy cried. "You can't stop them from killing me, any more than you could stop them from killing my cousin Rose."

Sammy's words cut through Slocum's heart like a hunk of lead from a .45. "They won't kill you," Slocum said. "Not if you trust me."

"And then what?" Sammy asked.

"We'll play it by ear," Slocum said. "Just like you do with your fiddle."

"From music I know, Mr. Slocum," Sammy said. "And this is one melody I don't want to play, if it's all the same to you."

Slocum tossed Sitting Duck the burlap sack full of Sammy's duds. He said, "Unpack this stuff, my friend. Mr. Kaminsky has decided to stay in our humble but fair town."

Slocum pulled out his pistol and replaced the three bul-lets he'd used to dispatch Flat Eye. He spun the chamber and said, "This is how we settle our differences out west, Sammy. Not a whole lot different from where you come from. I know. I've been there."

Sammy thought of his music-loving friend Monk Westman shooting one of his stooges in the knee that day in the clubhouse. Come to think of it, people *were* always shooting each other in Brooklyn. On the other hand, none of them had ever shot at him.

"I'm going to make a man out of you, Sammy," Slocum said. "I'll have to, if I ever want any peace of mind. You're going to stay alive and take what's rightfully yours by law—and I'm the law in Roseville. Hell, what are you worried about? It ain't like Potter's outside the door, waiting to kill you."

"How do you know?" Sammy asked.

"What am I, chopped liver?" Slocum said, remembering one of Rose's favorite expressions. "Sitting Duck, take a peek out the window and tell me if Potter is waiting out there to kill our friend here."

Sitting Duck dutifully went to the window and parted the curtains, peering outside.

"So what do you see? Nothing, of course," Slocum said.

Sitting Duck turned from the window and nodded at Slocum. He said, "Nothing."

"Happy?" Slocum said to Sammy, going into the kitchen for more coffee. "What are you worried about?"

"Nothing," Sitting Duck repeated. "Except for two of Potter's hired braves waiting across street."

Slocum went to the window, trying to look nonchalant. He drew his gun and parted the curtains with the barrel. Sure enough, two hardcases were leaning on either side of a walnut tree opposite Rose's house.

"That son of a bitch," Slocum muttered.

Sammy, by this time, had joined Slocum at the window. He swallowed and said, "Are they who I think they are?"

"They ain't here to pitch horseshoes," Slocum said. He

knew both. One was Otis Harper, a short, squat, nasty little toady who usually had his nose halfway up Potter's butt. The other was Happy Perkins, but there was nothing happy about him. Both rode shotgun for Potter. Not killers as killers went, really, but mean enough to be a problem. They would have to be dealt with.

"This is not high up on the list of things I like," Sammy said nervously.

"Mine either," Slocum said.

Sammy said, "Those are bad men, and with guns yet."

"Men, yes," Slocum said. "Bad—maybe. I think I have an idea." He went into the kitchen and brought back the bottle of whiskey. He handed it to the big Indian. "Think you could pretend to be a drunk?"

Sitting Duck uncorked the bottle and took a long swig. He said, "It be stretch, but I try."

Sitting Duck staggered down the street, clutching the bottle of whiskey. He made his way toward Harper and Perkins, swaying and singing drunkenly.

Harper and Perkins watched Sitting Duck come their way. Harper shook his head sadly and said, "Lookit that lousy redskin. Drunk as a skunk."

"Damned waste of good whiskey," Perkins agreed. "Think this low-down redskin would mind iffen we borrowed his bottle?"

"Shoot," Harper said. "I don't think he'll mind at all. Hey, redskin, y'all mind if we take that bottle?"

It may have been a question, but Harper didn't wait for an answer. He snatched the bottle, which was three-quarters full, from Sitting Duck and took a long swallow. Happy Perkins grabbed the bottle from Harper and did likewise.

"You git now," Harper commanded. "Back to the reservation."

Happy Perkins passed the bottle back to Harper, who said, "Sorta got me a hankerin' to kill something tonight."

Sitting Duck was gone by the time, having vanished

into the dark of night. Perkins chortled and said, "Guess you tol' him, Otis."

Harper said, "Indians oughtn't to drink whiskey. Makes 'em crazy."

A little later, just as the hardcases were finishing off the remains of the bottle, Sitting Duck appeared out of the still night, clutching a second bottle of whiskey. Harper took it away, and Sitting Duck disappeared once more.

An hour or so later, Harper and Perkins were taking potshots at the three empty whiskey bottles they'd set upon the fence across the street. Harper swigged from a fourth bottle, attempting to hit the third in a drunken haze. Happy Perkins was similarly soused. Sitting Duck was standing by with a fifth bottle, just in case. It was hardly necessary. For Perkins and Harper, standing was a Herculean task.

"Watch me get tha' little sum-bich this time," Harper slurred, and took his best shot, missing the bottle by a good three feet.

"I should like to maybe have a talk with you two gentlemen," came a voice from behind. Harper and Perkins wheeled around unsteadily to see Sammy standing fifteen feet away, with a cloth-covered basket on his arm.

"Well, looky what we-all got us here," Harper said drunkenly. "It's the little Yankee peckerwood."

Perkins squeezed off a shot that kicked up a small cloud of dust six inches from Sammy's left foot. Both men roared with laughter.

"You got vittles in that there basket?" Harper wanted to know.

Sammy shook his head. "No vittles. Just some food. Thought you gentlemen might like a little *nosh*."

Sammy lifted the cloth off the basket. Inside were a dozen or so overripe tomatoes.

"Tomatoes?" Happy Perkins asked indignantly. "We cain't eat no rotten tomatoes."

"They're not for eating," Sammy replied, and with one

quick motion, he plucked the biggest one from the basket and hurled it like a red cannonball at Harper. He scored a direct hit: The tomato exploded in Harper's ugly face.

Happy Perkins broke out in uproarious laughter as seeds and red pulp dripped from his partner's surprised face.

"He does better with veg-ables than you do with bullets, Otis," Happy Perkins said and guffawed. He turned to Sammy. "Boy, you got—"

Another tomato came out of nowhere and splattered in Happy Perkins's mug.

Harper started laughing this time. Happy Perkins barked, "Shut up, fool." To Sammy he said, "I'm gonna drill you six more assholes, Yankee."

"You should go, you'll pardon the expression, straight to hell," Sammy barked, and started flinging the tomatoes in earnest, advancing confidently toward them. Each tomato found its target, blinding them temporarily. His right arm was much stronger than his left as a result of years of violin practice, and even showed signs of an actual muscle.

Sammy flung the last tomato at Harper's head. Both men were wiping red slop from their eyes. Sammy dropped the basket and took the opportunity to rip the pistols from their hands.

"Everything with you *meshuga* Texas people is guns, guns, guns," Sammy said angrily. "How would you like it if I shot you in the *pipick* with this thing?" He jabbed Perkins in the belly with the barrel of the pistol. "These guns can hurt a person, for God's sake. They can kill you—and worse!"

Sammy felt an emotion something akin to rage bubbling in his blood. He said, "You're not happy beating me up and smashing my violin, now you want to kill me with these. What, you think this little vacation has been a barrel of herring for me? You'll forgive me, but I'm not liking this Texas very much."

Sammy spun on his heels and raised Harper's Colt revolver at the row of whiskey bottles on the fenceposts.

Though he had never even handled a gun before, much less shot one, Sammy nonetheless squeezed off three shots and skillfully blasted each bottle into tiny bits.

Watching from behind a barn, where he'd positioned himself so as to be close in case anything went wrong, Slocum's eyes widened in surprise as he watched Sammy hit all three bottles.

"Well, I'll be dipped in cowshit," Slocum muttered to himself. The kid was a natural.

Sammy, looking angrier than a swarm of wasps, a gun in each hand, put the barrel of one flat on Harper's nose, the barrel of the other on Happy Perkins's. They looked frightened.

"Now you two *shmendricks* leave me alone," Sammy said. "And the next time you feel like hurting people with guns, do yourself a big favor and have a nice tomato instead."

"Y-yes, sir," Harper stammered. He looked over at Happy Perkins, who nodded in agreement. Then they turned and bolted down the street faster than two farts in a Kansas twister.

Slocum came out from behind the barn. Sitting Duck emerged from behind a huge walnut tree in the front yard. They exchanged incredulous glances.

Slocum said to Sammy, who had begun to quake with delayed fear, "Well, shit on fire and save the matches, boy. Where'd you learn to shoot like that?"

"Shoot like what?" Sammy asked, confused.

"Hell, son," Slocum said. "You blasted all three bottles into little bits."

Sammy said, wide-eyed, "I did?"

Slocum came over to him. "Don't you remember, Sammy? You scared the living shit out of those tramps. Ran like their asses were on fire."

Sammy looked down with some surprise at the pistols still clenched in his fists. He said, "I guess I don't remember."

Slocum studied him carefully. Sammy's eyes were

glazed over; he wasn't quite himself. Slocum had seen the look before. It was the look of a man who'd just killed another.

Going for the guns in Sammy's hands, Slocum said, "Here, why don't you let me take those?"

"Let's go inside," Sammy said. "I think maybe it's time to be puttin' on the feedle-bag." He added thoughtfully, "Who knows, maybe I'll even have some bacon."

Slocum and Sitting Duck exchanged another glance, shrugged, and followed him inside.

12

"He hit you with *what*?" Potter thundered.

"Tomatoes, Boss," Happy Perkins said sheepishly.

They were in Potter's ranch headquarters. The sun was creeping up sluggishly in the eastern sky. With it came the promise of a beautiful spring day, but Potter was in no mood to enjoy it.

"You tellin' me that little bastard whopped you with tomatoes and you ran away?" Potter asked, not believing his hairy ears.

"You don't understand, Boss," Harper pleaded. The tomatoes had dried to a pink crust all over his pants and shirt and face. "That kid's got the eyes of a hawk when it comes to shootin'. He—"

"Shut the hell up, Otis," Happy Perkins snapped. "Next thing you'll be tellin' him how he took our guns away, so just—"

"He took your goddamn guns away?" Potter roared, and dove across his battered desk, grabbing Harper's throat. He sank his huge fingers into the tender flesh of Harper's neck. His eyes started bulging. Gregory and Al Bridge rushed to restrain Potter, pulling him away.

"He ain't worth killin', Eustace," Bridge said, trying to soothe the boss. "We'll think of something else."

Potter shook himself free.

"I already thunk it," he said, angrily. "We got to kill Slocum. He's the one what's keepin' the pot simmering. We make him go away, and the kid'll run for his life."

Potter came around from behind his desk and grabbed the collar of Happy Perkins's shirt. His teeth clenched, Potter said to Perkins, "Ever cut a dog's head off with a sharp knife?"

"Cain't say as I ever did, Boss," Perkins squeaked. He was having a very bad day.

"Funny thing," Potter said, his nose almost touching Happy's. "Slice off a pup's head and his tail just stops waggin'." He pushed Happy Perkins away and said to Al Bridge, "To hell with it all. I want them both dead."

"Now, Eustace," Bridge said, the voice of reason, "you know this ain't like the old days when you could slaughter anyone who didn't share your idears for the future."

He eased Potter into a chair next to the desk. No other man had the calming effect on Eustace Potter that Al Bridge did. The powerful rancher had been trusting his foreman's instincts for years and was always the better for it.

"Killin' Slocum and the kid will just make things hotter, Eustace," Bridge said. "No, there's a better way. We need to put some fear into the heart of our Yankee friend."

"We tried that last night," Potter said. "And it didn't work."

"I reckon we just didn't try hard enough, Eustace," Bridge said.

"What you got in mind, *compadre*?" Potter asked.

"I'm still studying on it," Bridge said. "But when I'm done, I think you'll like it."

"I damn well better," Potter said.

Dear Aunt Meema and Uncle Jake:

    I take my pencil in my hand to write to you today, to let you know that I am well, having survived my first week here none wear for the worse. I wish I could say the same for my violin.

This land called Texas is much different from Williamsburg. The people talk funny, they say things like "yall" and "howdy" and that they are "fixin" to do this and that. Strange indeed. Mr. Slocum has been very nice. He watches out for me and makes sure no harm comes to me. I can understand why cousin Rose liked him so much.

Texas is very hot and dusty, and there is a lot of open space. I never knew there were so many stars in heaven, a lot more than we ever saw on the rooftops of Brooklyn. And the air is different here in Texas than in New York. It doesn't smell and you can't see it. Except when the cafe serves something called "chili."

Mr. Slocum is teaching me to ride a horse. It's hard on the *tuchas* but is the only way to get from one place to another in a land where there are no trolleys. One horse tried to bite me yesterday. Mr. Slocum said that horses can smell fear. Mine smelled so bad I was surprised he could smell anything else. I can understand, though, why the horse wanted to *nosh* on my leg. How would you feel if a horse wanted to ride on you every day?

It appears that I have a talent for shooting guns. Some gentlemen who came to visit kindly loaned me some of theirs and I ended up shooting empty *schnapps* bottles off a fence. Mr. Slocum said I was a "crack shot." That means I'm fast. Mr. Slocum says I need to know how to use a gun, that everybody uses them in Texas. This is true, as Texans love their guns the way you love your lox and bagels, Uncle Jake. They carry them in belts called holsters, all out in the open, not like in New York where people hide them in their pants. Still, I am not so sure I like these guns. I've seen what they can do. Mr. Slocum said that a gun is the tool of the Devil in the hands of the wrong man, but that a man needs to have something called a "reputation" as a "gunslinger" before people will leave him alone. Damned if you do, damned if you don't, Mr. Slocum says. He is always saying odd things like that.

I met a nice woman named Louise who works for cousin Rose in one of her many businesses. Louise is very big-hearted and generous in her own way. I met another girl on the train named Emily, who was also very nice, but I do not know if I will see her again. She is marrying another man named Luke who is a cowboy in the employ of Mr. Potter, who runs a very large ranch. Mr. Potter owns a lot of land and has lots of money, more than anyone in the territory, but he is not a happy man. I do not think he likes me, though I did nothing to anger him.

I am eating well, Aunt Meema, so do not worry about that. I have been "taking my meals," as Mr. Slocum says, at the Roseville cafe. A lady named Miss Amelia does all the cooking. Mostly fried chicken and steak and potatoes and apple pie. At first, I thought I was sick after eating Miss Amelia's food, because there was no pain in my stomach afterwards. Not at all like your cooking, Aunt Meema. I have come to the conclusion that food does not have to hurt. I still miss your blintzes, though.

Cousin Rose's many businesses have been making a lot of money, much more than I know what to do with. Mr. Slocum has been helping me collect cousin Rose's earnings. I am arranging to transfer one thousand dollars to an account in your names at the Williamsburg Savings and Trust. There will be much more to come, Mr. Slocum says, so if you want, you can sell the restaurant and buy that house near the ocean in Coney Island you always dreamed of.

I will put my pencil down now in the hopes that you are both happy and in good health. I hope to be coming home just as soon as I can. There is much business to take care of first, Mr. Slocum says. In the meantime, I will seek my destiny, Uncle Jake. I do not know yet if

I like this Texas, but if this is where God wills me to be, than here is where I will stay.

Your loving nephew,
Samuel David Kaminsky

"So why exactly do you call it a 'barn dance'?" Sammy asked. "You dance with a barn maybe?"

Sitting next to Slocum in the wagon, Melody Daniels giggled. Sammy was wearing a suit several sizes too large that Slocum had chosen for him down at the mercantile. Unfortunately, it was the only suit that even remotely fit Sammy's slight stature.

"Not *with* a barn—*in* a barn," Slocum explained, steering the wagon. "That's why we call it a barn dance."

"What'll they think of next?" Sammy said. "Only in America."

"I'm sure you'll enjoy yourself, Mr. Kaminsky," Melody said, one hand on Slocum's knee.

"It all sounds very nice," Sammy said. "But I'm not sure why I need to go. I'm not a good dancer. In fact, I got two feet that couldn't help each other on a dance floor to save their lives."

"I told you before," Slocum said, snapping the whip at the horses' rumps. "It's important that you get to know the townfolk in Roseville. And they get to know you."

"And what if Mr. Potter shows up with his nasty friends, Mr. Smarty-Pants?" Sammy asked, each bounce in the wagon rattling his kidneys.

"Most likely he won't," Slocum answered. "And even if he does, Potter's not dumb enough to try anything in public." The back left wagon wheel hit a big rock in the road.

"No," Slocum said, as the Pendergast barn appeared on the horizon. The annual Fourth of July celebration at Tom Pendergast's barn had been a tradition in the territory for twenty years. "Potter'll sooner back-shoot you tomorrow than risk dozens of witnesses seeing him plug you tonight."

"If you're trying to make me feel better, Mr. Slocum," Sammy said, "there's room for improvement."

"Relax, boy," Slocum said. "Just stay real close and have yourself some fun."

Privately, Slocum didn't quite believe his own words. Potter was a ruthless man and not afraid, as he had demonstrated, to kill anyone who dared awaken him from his dreams of owning the entire territory. Nonetheless, Slocum reasoned, for Sammy to hide from Potter was worse.

"Sammy," Slocum said, "you got to understand the ways of men like Eustace Potter. You run for cover and Potter won't have any respect for you."

"The man turns my violin into toothpicks and sends bad men to hurt me," Sammy said. "I don't think respecting Samuel Kaminsky is high up on his list of things to worry about."

"Let us not forget, Master Kaminsky, that you own most of Roseville and half the ranchers in this piece of Texas."

"I don't want to own anything," Sammy said. "I just want to go back to Brooklyn."

"That's not the way Rose wanted it," Slocum said. "She left you this town, and you're taking it."

"Couldn't I just sign a short-term lease?" Sammy asked. "Listen, Mr. Slocum. I'm a little nebbish from New York, not a sling-gunner. *You* should have the town. You knew my cousin Rose a lot better than I did. She was your friend, you cared for her. You deserve Roseville more than I do. So take it, and God bless."

"Like I said," Slocum said. "That ain't the way Rose wanted it." The Pendergast ranch loomed closer. Dozens of wagons were already pulled up and being tended to by Sitting Duck. Inside the barn, raucous music was blaring. Slocum said, "Believe me, the townfolk don't want to see Roseville fall into Potter's hands any more than you do."

"That's nice," Sammy said sourly.

13

Inside the Pendergast barn, the good people of Roseville were busy square-dancing, socializing, and drinking lemonade that came in two flavors—spiked and unspiked.

Abraham Lincoln Botts was pounding the piano keys, leading the other musicians—Pete Fawcett, the blacksmith, on the fiddle; Isaiah Graves, the town mortician, on the washboard; and Ferd Olsen, the barber, on the mouth organ.

Once inside, Slocum took Miss Melody and off across the dance floor they went. Sammy, left to his own devices, took in the spectacle. These Texas people danced a lot different from the Jews in Williamsburg, not that Sammy had much experience dancing. This was limited mostly to weddings, where the men danced with one another while the women sat at tables and gossiped. The smell of horse poop permeated the barn, though nobody seemed to care.

Behind Sammy was a table covered with a punch bowl, a dozen apple pies, and platters of barbecue. A stout woman with her gray hair tied back in a severe bun, her face brown and weathered like a dried-up pretzel, grinned at Sammy from ear to ear.

"I'm Lila Pendergast," the old woman said, extending a hand calloused from years of hard ranch life. "You must be Mr. Kaminsky. We've all been looking forward to meeting you. Some lemonade?"

"Yes, thank you," Sammy said. Mrs. Pendergast handed him a cup full of the yellow liquid. Sammy sniffed it suspiciously.

"Go ahead, drink," Mrs. Pendergast urged. "Nothin' but lemons and water and a touch of the hair of the dog."

"There's dog hair in this?" Sammy asked with distaste.

Mrs. Pendergast chuckled. Sammy shrugged and downed the punch in one gulp. It felt like liquid flame sliding down his throat. Sammy coughed until his face turned the color of ripe radishes. Mrs. Pendergast cackled and took the glass. She dipped it into the bowl and scooped out more.

"Ain't never sampled no Texas champagne, have you, son?" she asked.

"I don't suppose I have," Sammy said, getting his breath back. "But I don't drink from oil lamps, either."

Mrs. Pendergast cackled and handed Sammy the filled glass. "Maybe not, son," she said, "but we're gonna get you lit all the same."

Sammy took a small sip. It went down much easier this time; his eyes didn't water. The *schnapps* in the lemonade tasted good. No wonder Aunt Meema never let him have any when Uncle Jake and his friends drank the stuff, while playing cards in the kitchen, in their undershirts. Aunt Meema hated anything that might be fun. "If we spent all our lives having fun," Aunt Meema was fond of saying, "so tell me, when would we have time to suffer?"

So what the hell, Sammy thought, and downed the rest. His head felt hot, and for a few seconds his dinner wanted to come up. He fought it back down.

"Best go a mite easier," Mrs. Pendergast warned.

Sammy grinned crookedly and handed her the glass. "I would be very obliged if all-you would be hankering to be fixing to give me another."

Mrs. Pendergast did just that. Handing him the glass, she said, "Your cousin was a fine woman, Mr. Kaminsky, even if she was a fallen one. Could have foreclosed on us anytime she wanted, but she didn't. Always cut us some slack, she did. Believed in people first; money came second. A good lady she was."

"And look where it got her," Sammy said, slurring his words. His tongue felt thicker than a slab of pastrami. "Doorer than a deadnail."

Slocum and Miss Melody came waltzing by. Slocum said to Mrs. Pendergast, "Don't let him drink too much of that stuff, Lila. It'll go straight to his head."

"I suspect it already has," Mrs. Pendergast said.

By now, the other townsfolk and ranchers had gravitated toward Sammy and were heartily introducing themselves. Sammy's head started spinning as dozens of dusty, weathered people came over to pay their respects to the scrawny, pale Yankee who was the heir to Miss Rose's fortune, not to mention holding mortgages on most of them. Sammy was invited to barbecues, church suppers, and afternoon teas.

Sammy drank more lemonade and chatted with the good people of Roseville. Everything seemed right with the world.

Slocum and Miss Melody continued dancing, watching as Sammy was welcomed to the town. He said, "That skinny little *schlemiel* may survive out here yet."

"I think he'll be just fine, John," Miss Melody said, gripping his hands a little more tightly as they waltzed.

Abraham Lincoln Botts stroked the last few keys of the waltz. He stood and went over to Pete Fawcett, the fiddle player.

"Mind if I borry this for a spell, Mr. Fawcett?" Abe asked. He took the fiddle and the bow and weaved his way through the crowd. He handed them to Sammy and said, "I'd be honored if you accompanied me and the others in a little ditty, Mr. Sammy."

To the cheers of the townspeople, Sammy took the

violin and followed Abe back to the makeshift stage. This appeared to be the largest audience he'd ever performed for, except for maybe the customers at Uncle Jake's restaurant—most of whom ignored him.

Abe sat down at the piano and ripped into a tune Sammy had never heard before, singing about a camptown racetrack being five miles long, do-dah, do-dah. Sammy did his best to fiddle along in time with the others. If he played a little sour, the townsfolk didn't seem to care, dancing up a storm as fast as Abe and Sammy could play. Slocum, Sammy saw, was quite the dancer, skillfully twirling Miss Melody across the dirt floor. The mood in the place—or Sammy's, anyway—was as light as a feather.

Sammy stroked the strings and watched as a familiar man, accompanied by an older woman and a younger one in a pretty yellow bonnet, entered the barn.

It wasn't until the young lady took off the bonnet and shook her silky yellow hair that Sammy recognized her. It was Miss Emily Shields, the one from the train.

Sammy watched as she greeted the townsfolk then went over and said something to Mrs. Pendergast.

Mrs. Pendergast pointed to the stage. Sammy saw Miss Emily turn and look at him and smile from ear to ear. Sammy smiled back, still playing but missing every other note. Abe saw the reason why, and pounded the keys harder to cover Sammy's mistakes.

"Mighty fine little lady, that Miss Emily," Abe commented.

"Yes, she is," Sammy said.

Miss Emily pushed her way through the crowd to stand a few feet away from Sammy.

"It's nice to see you again, Mr. Kaminsky," she said above the racket. "I hope you're well."

Sammy heard only every other word. "Yes, it's been hell," he yelled back, nodding.

"I was hoping I'd run into you again," Emily said when they finished playing.

"To be completely honest, I was sort of hoping you wouldn't," Sammy said.

Emily looked puzzled, then hurt. "Why do you say that?"

"I don't think your cowboy friend liked me too much," Sammy said, "and if he saw me talking to you, or you talking to me, well, I've had enough hurt in the last few weeks to last me ten lifetimes."

"You needn't worry about Mr. Luke Price," Emily sniffed. "I have broke my engagement with him after his despicable treatment of you at the train station."

"I'm sorry to hear that," Sammy lied, drowning in her sea-green eyes. She was the prettiest girl he'd ever seen, he decided there and then. "Was that the only reason?"

"No," she said. "There was another. I didn't love him."

"Now that's a very good reason."

"I would be grateful, Mr. Kaminsky," Emily said, "if you would save a dance for me."

"For you I'll save them all," Sammy said.

As if on cue, Abe Botts appeared next to Sammy and gently plucked the fiddle from his hand. Sammy handed Abe the bow, his eyes never leaving Emily's. Abe gave the fiddle back to Fawcett and the music started anew.

Sammy felt himself floating down off the stage toward Emily Shields. She looked very happy to see him. Sammy felt the same lurching in his belly as he had the day he'd met her on the train to Killeen. His first instinct was to take her in his arms and sweep her off her feet across the barn floor. Then Sammy dimly remembered that he didn't know how to dance.

Emily saw his hesitation. She guessed that this New Yorker had never used his feet for anything other than walking. She went to him and took his hands in hers, so they were facing each other a foot or so apart.

"Have you ever do-si-do'd before?" she asked.

"Do-si-do'd?" This was a very difficult question. Sammy remembered his one encounter with Louise at the whorehouse and the several awkward and unsatisfying attempts at consummating their union. Sammy wasn't entirely sure he'd actually "sank the big salami" with her, as the other boys in Brooklyn described it.

"I think I did once," Sammy stammered, "but I'm not sure." He felt his face flush.

"Maybe I can teach you proper-like," Emily offered.

"Here?" Sammy asked, his eyebrows rising half an inch. "Now?"

"As good a place as any, I suspect," Emily said, grinning.

Sammy had heard Slocum comment about the wide, open spaces in Texas, but this wasn't what he had imagined. A bead of sweat rolled down between his shoulder blades.

"Maybe we should instead dance," he said meekly.

"Of course we'll dance," Emily said indignantly. "What did you think I was talking about, Mr. Kaminsky?" She looked at him suspiciously now.

Sammy felt his armpits dripping. These Texas women, he thought. They confused a person until he was crazy in the head. He said, "You should excuse me if I don't have the slightest idea. From do-si-do's I know *bupkus*."

"Just take two steps to the left, two steps to the right, and try to do it in time to the music," she said.

"Of course," Sammy said, nodding vigorously. "From music I understand, from Professor Stossel."

Slowly, awkwardly, with Miss Emily as his teacher, Sammy half waltzed, half stumbled along to something that sort of resembled actual dancing. He was vaguely aware as some men he hadn't seen before began filtering into the barn, though Miss Emily was swinging him back and forth across the floor so fast, everything was a boozy blur.

Suddenly he felt rough hands jerk him backward, out of Miss Emily's grasp, then spin him around. When Sammy finally focused, he saw Luke Price, Miss Emily's former fiancé, glaring at him. Hatred, pure and simple, blazed from the narrow slits that were Luke Price's eyes.

The sight sobered Sammy in seconds. His throat twitched convulsively. The music had suddenly stopped, and Sammy could feel the eyes of every man, woman, and child in the barn on him. Where was Slocum?

"You stole my gal," Luke Price said, his teeth clenched. "You know what we do to Yankee trash what tries to steal our women?"

Sammy, his eyes wider than the Hudson River, blinked nervously and said, "Could I maybe sleep on it?"

Price growled deep in his throat and started advancing toward Sammy, pulling a knife along the way. Sammy had no way of seeing Slocum skulk up behind him.

Luke Price, for his part, had only one true goal in life: to gut this Yankee boy from neck to nuts. He stopped abruptly when he saw Slocum looming tall behind the Yankee. Slocum was shaking his head at Luke as if to say, *Not today, shithead.*

"Stand up to him, boy," Slocum said in Sammy's ear. "You got no choice."

"So tell me something I don't know," Sammy said.

Sammy clenched his fists, but wasn't quite sure what to do with them. He knew one or the other or perhaps both should be pummeling Price; it was the distance between his fists and Price's head that momentarily baffled him.

In a shining example of perfect timing, Al Bridge pushed through the crowd surrounding both men. He grabbed Price's arm just as Sammy, catching Price off his guard, put every ounce of weight he had into a well-placed haymaker that connected with Price's jaw.

Price fell backward into Bridge's arms, knocked silly, and a hush came over the good people of Roseville. Sammy looked in wonderment at his fist, as though it had just grown out of his shoulder that morning.

Price recovered quickly from the blow and tried to lunge at Sammy. Bridge held tight and hissed low in Price's ear, "Now ain't the time, I done told you that before. You'll get your chance later."

Bridge started to drag Price, who was snorting like a

furious boar, toward the barn door.

Bridge said, "Sorry for the interruption, folks," and shoved Price outside.

Slocum slapped Sammy on the back, then everyone else in Roseville followed suit, congratulating him for knocking Luke Price down. Men grasped his hand and took turns shaking it. Sammy looked at Slocum, puzzled.

"Did I just do what I think I just did?" Sammy asked.

"You flattened the little bastard, that's what you did," Slocum said with a grin.

"I made him flat?" Sammy asked, and again looked at his fist in amazement.

"Sure as shit," Slocum said.

Slocum knew, of course, that fate, in the form of Al Bridge, as much as Sammy's punch, had felled Luke Price. But Slocum chose to ignore this fact, knowing that Sammy needed confidence, maybe enough to fill the Pacific.

"I've never hit anyone in my life," Sammy said, sounding alarmed.

"First time for everything, boy," Slocum said.

Sammy looked over at Miss Emily, who was smiling with something like love in her pretty eyes.

Someone thrust a cup of ninety-proof lemonade into Sammy's hand and he downed it in one gulp. Somebody else thoughtfully handed him another.

Sammy downed this one as well, never taking his eyes off Miss Emily. He felt something burning deep inside him, though this feeling was different from the heartburn he got from a breakfast of fried salami and eggs. Sammy wanted to punch someone else, then drag Miss Emily into a corner and kiss every inch of her face and much, much more.

Miss Emily took Sammy's hand in hers. Abe Botts saw this as his cue to start the music again. Miss Emily glided with Sammy across the barn floor.

"Yes, I'd say our new friend is beginning to fit in nicely," Miss Melody commented to Slocum. They were standing on the other side of the barn floor, nibbling on sugar cookies.

Slocum watched Sammy being dragged around the barn by Emily Shields, his step a little unsteady. Slocum had no doubt that Sammy had consumed more alcohol in one hour than in his whole life up to now.

"Yes," Slocum said. "Though he ain't out of the woods yet."

Melody looked concerned. "What do you mean, John?" she asked.

"Let's just wait and see," Slocum said. "And now, my dear Miss Melody," he added, taking her dainty hand and kissing it, "I must respectfully excuse myself, as I need to answer nature's call, as all men must."

"You mean y'all got to pee," Melody said dryly.

"Yes," Slocum said, taking his leave, "and right badly."

Slocum made his way into the night, heading toward the outhouse. He was a little drunk his own self. He'd sworn off the stuff after his last binge, but he'd relaxed his self-imposed liquor law to include barn dances and special occasions. Of course, every day held the promise of a special occasion if a man relaxed enough.

The outhouse wasn't hard to find. A shape like a half moon had been sliced from the wooden door. Slocum ambled over to it, and luckily, it was unoccupied. He stepped inside and started to do what came naturally.

He was shaking off the last few drops when he felt the gun metal jab his spine.

"One move and I'll blow your butt off," someone growled behind him. Slocum quickly identified the voice; it belonged to Happy Perkins.

"Ain't your gun a little high up for that, Hap?" Slocum asked.

"Big joke," he heard Perkins snarl.

Something hard came down on the back of Slocum's skull, and the last thing he remembered was spiraling down to the splintered wooden outhouse floor.

• • •

Sammy's head was spinning faster than his feet.

Emily was quite the dancer and was doing her damnedest to make Sammy into one. He was doing pretty well, she thought, keeping up with her, though all the spiked lemonade had taken a toll on him. He was stepping on her feet more often than he wasn't. She didn't mind. She'd teach him proper in the time to come.

Sammy, for his part, was having a spectacular time. He'd gotten drunk, danced with a beautiful woman, and punched someone—all in the space of one evening. More and more he was beginning to like this Texas.

His inhibitions six sheets to the wind, Sammy swung Miss Emily around and cried out to Abe Botts, "Abraham, my friend, give me a bouncy chord of C."

Abe started bouncing a C off the barn walls, and Sammy taught the folks of Roseville how to dance Jewish wedding style, locking arms with Miss Emily and her father both and dancing them forward and backward, kicking his legs toward heaven. They tried in vain to keep up with him, but Sammy wasn't to be held back by anyone, as the rhythm and the liquor took over and possessed him to dance as his ancestors had danced in the old country. He was dimly aware of people clapping, egging him on.

He continued to dance, sweating like a herring in August. Abe pounded the piano keys harder and Sammy danced and sweated harder. Suddenly, like a lightning bolt, he felt dizzy and tried to fight down an overwhelming need to throw up. He stopped dancing abruptly and ran from the barn, his stomach doing backflips. He clamped his hand over his mouth until he was a safe distance from the barn, behind a junked wagon with no wheels.

He took his hand away from his mouth and let loose everything in his stomach—including a lunch he'd eaten when he was twelve—too late to notice the spit-shined pair of boots standing before him. Sammy vomited all over them, then looked up to see that Luke Price was standing inside the boots. He didn't look happy.

Standing on either side of Price were Al Bridge and Eustace Potter and some of their men. They didn't look happy, either. They looked like they wanted Sammy to be dead, as if they resented him breathing their air.

Luke Price looked down at his puke-splattered boots, then looked at Sammy.

"You done barfed on mah boots, boy," he said. He looked at Sammy again, way past angry now. Instead, he looked almost serene, as though Sammy's painful death were a given, almost an afterthought.

"I guess saying I'm sorry is out of the question," Sammy said.

Price's response came in the form of a hard belt from his fist, into Sammy's nose. Blood gushed from his crushed nostrils and he staggered backward against the side of the wagon. He tried to stand, and a boot, someone else's, came out of the darkness and slammed into his belly.

Sammy crashed back against the wagon, landing flat on his ass. Blood from his nose cascaded into his hand. He didn't know where to hurt first.

Luke Price reached down and grabbed Sammy by the collar of his shirt and yanked him up.

"I'm gonna beat your skinny ass six ways from Sunday," Price said, and smacked Sammy a second time in the bread basket.

Sammy doubled over and let loose with a second stream of puke. This one, too, splattered on Price's boots.

For the second time that night, Sammy wondered where Slocum was. Wherever he was, it was the wrong place.

Price looked down again at his boots, covered with Sammy's steaming innards. He lashed out with a solid uppercut to Sammy's chin. Sammy's head snapped back like the cap off a bottle of celery tonic, and down he went. He was roughly dragged to his feet by Price, and Potter and Bridge and their stooges descended on him, punching him in the head and the chest and the midsection.

He crashed to the ground, and they viciously kicked him in the ribs and the crotch, until his entire body was one big mass of pain. Then, just as quickly as it had started, the attack ended, and not a moment too soon.

A huge shadow fell over Sammy, who was struggling to stay conscious. Sammy looked up into the black, lifeless eyes of Eustace Potter, who towered above him. He was a safe distance away, lest Sammy's stomach erupt once more.

"I ain't gonna warn you again," Potter croaked. "I'm a-gonna give you the chance to go home in one piece this time. So you get, boy, go back east, and don't let me see your ass for the dust."

Sammy tried to breathe. Each attempt was a new adventure in pain. Blood oozed from his split lower lip, in addition to the blood that was coursing from his shattered nose.

Sammy, lying in the dirt, clutching his sides, coughed up more blood. He said, "I seem to have angered you gentlemen."

They descended on him once more, kicking every square inch of his body, and after a while Sammy gave up and became unconscious. It was a much better place.

14

Slocum struggled back to consciousness. When he came fully awake, he didn't like what he saw: hay and lots of it, scratching his face and tickling his nose. He was lying facedown in a stack of the stuff, his wrists tied together tightly behind his back. His ankles were similarly bound.

He stirred, trying to wriggle free. Two barrels from a shotgun were instantly pressed against the back of his head.

"You stay put, Slocum," he heard Happy Perkins say. "I got me orders to kill you iffen you give me a lick of trouble."

"Wouldn't dream of it," Slocum muttered, the pain in his head scrambling his brains. Sunshine was streaming through the wooden planks of the roof above him. It was tomorrow, meaning he'd been out since last night and no mistake. "Where am I?"

"Hog-tied in my barn," said the gravelly, unmistakable voice of Eustace Potter. "Sit him up, Hap. I want to look the man straight in the eye."

Perkins grabbed Slocum by the hair and jerked him into a sitting position, and not gently. Slocum made mental note to kill Perkins sometime in the future, preferably sooner than later.

Slocum was plunked back onto his butt in the hay pile. Potter stood ten or so feet away, working on a wad of tobacco. He spit a stream of brown juice into the hay inches from where Slocum sat.

"Where's the boy?" Slocum asked, his eyes granite. "You kill him?"

"No, but he'll not be forgettin' me anytime soon," Potter said.

"You hurt him, Potter," Slocum said, "and I'll hurt you back twice as bad."

"Ain't got no argument with you, Slocum," Potter said, spitting again. "But it's my opinion y'all chose the wrong side."

"I reckon that's my affair, Potter," Slocum said. He could feel fresh blood trickle from the hole in the back of his head, also courtesy of Happy Perkins.

At that point, Potter growled, "Bring him in, boys." Two of Potter's men carried in a big bundle and dropped it at Slocum's feet. Slocum blinked a few times before he realized it was the lifeless body of Sitting Duck lying before him. There was a round, red bullet hole squarely between his eyes, which were still open.

"You stinkin', yellow bastard," Slocum hissed at Potter.

"Listen to me, Slocum," Potter said. "You want to keep healthy, stay out of my way. I got me some plans, friend, and neither you nor that Yankee boy figure in 'em."

"I know what y'all are up to, Potter," Slocum said. "And you ain't going to pull it off. This town belongs to Sammy Kaminsky, and you ain't taking it. Not while I'm alive."

"Have it your own way," Potter said. "But you keep one thing in mind, Slocum. I could've killed you at any time, whenever it met my fancy. But I didn't. You're breathin' now, and you got me to thank for it."

"How do I express my gratitude?" Slocum asked sarcastically.

Potter shook his head sadly. "Like I said, Slocum. Weren't for me, you'd be wakin' up with the angels right about now."

"Ain't that something," Slocum said.

"Be nice to me," Potter said, "and I'll be nice to you when the tide starts turnin' around here."

"And when is that supposed to happen?" Slocum wanted to know.

"Just wait and see." Potter turned and said to Happy Perkins, "Keep a close eye on him. Don't want him getting loose, unnerstand?"

"Sure, Boss," Perkins said.

"Could use a good man like you, Slocum," Potter said. "We could make some real money in this territory."

"I'd rather eat dirt," Slocum said.

"You keep playin' on the wrong side," Potter said, "and you'll be sleepin' in it, forever."

Potter turned and left. Slocum said to Happy Perkins, "I don't think he likes me."

Happy shrugged. Slocum might as well have been talking to a tree.

By sundown, Potter and his wolf pack had taken Roseville by storm, managing, with little trouble, to intimidate every business in town into splitting their profits in return for protection—from Potter.

His first stop was the whorehouse. Esther Howard, not surprisingly, welcomed Potter with open arms—and open legs. Since Rose's death, Slocum had kept a watchful eye on the slippery Miss Howard, ensuring that she deposited each day's earnings in the bank. Rose had kept good records, so Slocum knew, within a dollar or two, what the whorehouse pulled in. This alone kept Esther honest.

So it was no surprise that Esther cheerfully agreed to split the take with Potter—her half would still be more than she made running the place and from what she could skim when Rose was alive.

One by one, every business in town fell to Potter's threats: the hotel, the cafe, the mercantile, all of Rose's saloons, the blacksmith's, and every other establishment in town. Those who balked, such as Mr. Drake who owned Drake's Bakery, were mercilessly beaten, Drake in front of his wife and children. The smarter businessmen in town quickly came into line; there was no way they could stand up to Potter's two dozen men and their sixty guns.

Potter's deadly tentacles reached outside of town, as well. With the cooperation of Rose's unscrupulous partner in the Roseville Savings and Loan, Sam Dumbrille, Potter foreclosed on half the ranches in the territory that had notes with the bank. His hired guns, imported from as far away as Tucson to the west and Kansas City to the north, helped run the ranchers and their families off.

Among the ranches that Potter tried to seize was the Bar-S. Stanley Shields and his sons, Billy and Elmer, made the mistake of putting up a fight, with all the lead trimmings. The Shields men fought hard, killing two of Potter's boys and wounding three others, but at a huge cost. Billy Shields took a bullet in the gut and wasn't expected to survive the night.

Potter had set his plan into motion the moment Slocum was under wraps and the Yankee boy laid up with any number of injuries. Potter had gleefully watched him cough up blood. The Yankee was no longer a problem, with or without the help of John Slocum.

By the time the sun sank under the dry, dusty west Texas horizon, Eustace Potter was a much richer man. He sat atop his chestnut at the west end of Main Street, which afforded him an unobstructed view of the setting sun. Al Bridge on his mount sat beside him.

"Took us twenty years, Al," Potter said. "But it done looks like we finally got what we wanted."

Bridge grunted noncommittally. He thought of Slocum, hog-tied but still very much alive in the old barn outside of town. He'd urged his old friend to kill Slocum, but Potter had refused, insisting that Slocum would come around to their way of thinking sooner or later and could prove to be an asset to their organization. Bridge wasn't convinced. Slocum was a man of honor, and honor tended to die hard.

"We'll see, Eustace," Bridge said finally. "We'll see."

"Ain't very Christian," Slocum said to Happy Perkins and Otis Harper. "Not lettin' a man do as nature dictates."

"Shut up," Otis Harper said, chewing on a piece of hay. "Go pee-daddle in yer pants iffen you got to go so bad." Happy Perkins earned his nickname by laughing at his friend's rare display of wit. Sitting Duck's body, mercifully, had been taken away.

"The boot were on the other foot," Slocum said, still bound by the hands and ankles and lying facedown in the haystack, "I'd let you up to drain your lizard."

"Mr. Potter wouldn't approve," Perkins said, loading bullets into the chamber of his six-shooter.

"Mr. Potter don't have to know," Slocum said. "Just untie my wrists and help me over to the corner so's I can piss like a man was meant to. I won't give you no trouble, I swear."

"You must think we're pretty stupid, Slocum," Harper said, whittling on a chunk of wood. "Potter wants you hog-tied for a reason. Don't know why—I ain't a-feared of you—but orders is orders."

"If you ain't afraid of me, why don't you let me take a piss?" Slocum said. "A man holdin' his dick in his hand ain't no match for another holdin' a gun."

Happy Perkins thought this was funny. He said, "Sure, Otis. Your Peacemaker agin his piss-maker."

"Come on, Otis," Slocum said. "You had a dick, maybe you'd understand."

Happy Perkins laughed and said, "He got you there, Otis."

Otis Harper got mad. He hated it when people laughed at things he didn't understand but knew were directed at him. He put the barrel of his gun against the back of Slocum's head.

He said, "I could blow your head off, then you wouldn't have to worry 'bout takin' no piss."

"This is true," Slocum said. "But I don't think Potter would take kindly to it. He wants me alive, and he wants me alive with all my piss pipes in good workin' order."

Harper glanced over at Happy Perkins, who shrugged as if to say, *Let the man take a squirt.* Perkins said, "What the hell, he ain't goin' nowheres."

Harper holstered his pistol and grabbed the collar of Slocum's shirt. He dragged Slocum to his feet and shoved him toward the corner of the barn. He said, "Go piss, Slocum, and make it quick."

"You might try freein' my hands so I can unbutton my pants," Slocum said. "Unless you want to take it out for me."

Harper looked at him, cold steel in his eyes, and said, "You mess with me an' I'll blast you outta yer boots."

He untied Slocum's wrists. Slocum weaved back and forth, his ankles still bound together, and ended up leaning against the barn wall.

"I can't do what I got to do swaying to and fro," Slocum said. Harper sighed in exasperation and held Slocum steady by the collar. Slocum dutifully unbuttoned his pants and did what came naturally.

"Hurry up, Slocum," Harper snapped, the gun still pointed at the back of Slocum's head. "I ain't got all day."

Slocum hadn't been completely lying; his bladder had been swollen. He finished, and started buttoning his pants. A second later, he started howling in pain, grabbing his crotch.

"Jesus Christ," Slocum bellowed, and fell to the ground. "I'm stuck! Help me, for God's sake help me." Slocum wrestled with the buttons on his pants, rolling around in agony. "Untie my ankles so's I can loosen my britches."

Happy Perkins and Otis Harper looked at each other frantically. They could relate to Slocum's dilemma, having experienced it many times themselves. Perkins dropped to his knees and undid the ropes around Slocum's ankles, not sure why this would make any difference but doing it anyway.

Slocum continued howling in pain, clutching his privates. Harper and Perkins stood over him, contemplating Slocum's painful situation.

"What do we do?" Perkins asked.

"What the hell you askin' me for?" Harper said testily.

"Oh, sweet Jesus, help me," Slocum cried, rolling around on the dirt barn floor.

"They're his balls, they're his problem," Harper said.

Perkins thought this was funny, too, and started guffawing. Harper had never met anyone who got as much amusement out of the predicaments of everyday living. Even hiccups made Perkins hysterical.

He continued chortling. Otis Harper looked at his friend skeptically. Hap was a half-wit.

Slocum managed to stand, and minced around the barn wailing in agony and still clutching his groin.

"I'd say that man's in a downright prickly situation," Happy Perkins said.

Perkins and Harper helplessly followed behind Slocum at a safe distance, wondering how to help. Slocum saved them the trouble.

Leaning against the wall of the barn a few feet away from the hayloft was a huge metal shovel that easily weighed fifteen pounds. Slocum, still moaning in pain, stumbled over to it. He prayed that neither Perkins nor Harper noticed it.

The shovel was six feet away. Slocum staggered closer. Four feet. Three feet. Then: "Oh, no, bright boy," he heard Harper say from behind him. Harper dashed to the wall and grabbed the shovel before Slocum could get to it.

"I knows what you got on your mind, friend," Harper said triumphantly, holding the shovel over his head, away from Slocum.

Slocum spun around, and said, "The hell you do, friend."

He kicked out the pointy toe of his boot and connected perfectly between Harper's legs. Harper doubled over with a loud groan. Happy Perkins stood by dumbly, his mouth agape. It dimly occurred to him that this was very amusing, and he started laughing at his friend's agony.

Harper growled in anger and, clutching the shovel, came up and swung it as hard as he could at Slocum's head. Slocum neatly ducked, and the end of the shovel struck Perkins square in the face.

Perkins looked dazed for a moment, then crossed his eyes and fell flat on his back.

Harper's jaw dropped in horror at what he had done to his friend, who was out colder than a Wyoming winter.

"Jeez, Hap. I'm sorr—" Harper cried, stunned. Slocum plucked the shovel from Harper and crowned him, hitting his thick noggin so hard that Slocum could feel the handle of the shovel vibrate in his hands. Harper pitched forward in a crazy somersault before collapsing.

Some things, Slocum mused, were easier than others.

He set to work hog-tying both men, though both would be down for the count for a good two or three hours each. He wrapped up a pretty little package for Potter to find.

Outside the barn, Slocum untethered one of his captor's horses and slapped it hard on the rump. The horse trotted away in fear. He mounted the other, a sturdy bay, and rode off toward town.

15

Sammy said, "Do I look as bad as I feel?"

"Try not to talk, honey," Miss Melody said soothingly, dabbing his face with a cool, wet cloth.

Sammy was lying in Miss Melody's feather bed so that she could tend to him properly. The town sawbones, Doc Phipps, had been by the night before. Except for some bruised ribs, two split lips, two black eyes, a possible concussion, a possible fractured bone in his left arm, and pain in just about every major organ, Doc Phipps had pronounced Sammy battered but otherwise okay; he'd live, but he wouldn't be attending barn dances anytime soon. Doc Phipps had taped Sammy's injuries; Sammy's face was crisscrossed with the stuff. As a little icing on the cake, Potter had smashed Sammy's left hand with the heel of his boot, snapping his index finger. Phipps had taped and splinted this as well.

The events of the night before, to both Melody and Emily Shields, who was now in Melody's kitchen, fixing some soup for Sammy, were a little hazy. Both women had ventured out of the barn after Potter and his men had cleared out, looking for their men. They found Sammy with little problem, lying facedown, bloodied and barely conscious. Slocum was nowhere to be found, and Melody was assuming the worst.

"Where's Mr. Slocum?" Sammy asked weakly. His throat felt dryer than an ironing board.

"Can't say as I know," Melody said. She sounded worried.

"Did they kill him?" Sammy asked, every inch of his body in pain.

"Not likely," came Slocum's voice from the bedroom doorway.

Melody rushed to him and embraced him. Even Sammy managed a small smile.

"Oh, John—" Melody started to say, but Slocum's attention was riveted to the battered body on the bed. Sammy's eyes were puffy slits, his face a purple nightmare. There seemed to be white tape over half of it. He looked like he'd tried to stop a cattle stampede and lost.

"Sweet Jesus," Slocum muttered, going to the bed. "Shit on fire and save the matches, what in God's name did they do to you?"

"Use your imagination, then make it ten times worse," Sammy said weakly.

"Bastards," Slocum hissed. "Dirty, stinkin' miserable low-down, two-bit, double-shuffle, thimble-ringin', shit-suckin', rat-prick scum."

"You're being kind," Sammy said.

Slocum pulled up a chair and sat beside the bed.

"They bushwhacked me in the shitter," Slocum said, feeling as though some sort of explanation were necessary. He tried not to stare at Sammy's face. "Hog-tied me in a barn. All night."

"Things haven't been exactly a bed of blintzes for me, either," Sammy said.

Melody went to Sammy and gently dabbed his face cuts with a damp cloth. Emily came in carrying a bowl of soup on a tray. She sat on the edge of the bed and tried to feed him some, but Sammy could slurp down only a few spoonfuls of the beef broth.

"Maybe later," he said to her, waving the next spoonful away. "I don't suppose you know how to make a matzo ball?"

"This is all my fault," Slocum said. "I should've let you go home when you wanted. Should've known this was a losin' battle."

"You did the best you could, Mr. Slocum," Sammy said. "To speak God's truth, I think the odds were against us from the start."

"Potter's taking it," Slocum said now. "Everything Rose built. By tomorrow, he'll have it all. The bank, the whorehouse, the works." He got up and started pacing nervously. "We're beat and he knows it. You'll get better and hightail it out of here, and who could blame you? I was a dope to think I could keep the lid on things here, and a bigger dope to make you try and help me."

Slocum sat back down and looked at Sammy's ravaged face.

"Let's just get you well," Slocum said, "and send you back where you belong."

"Texas is where I belong," Sammy said. His vision was blurry, he struggled to see only one Slocum. He tried to lift his head off the pillow, but it made him dizzy. He slumped back with a painful sigh. "I don't know why, Mr. Slocum, but it took getting beaten half to death—no, make that three-quarters—to realize you were right."

"What the hell was I ever right about?" Slocum wanted to know.

"My cousin Rose left this town to me, and not so Mr. Fancy-Pants Potter could take it away." He swallowed painfully and said, "Could I have a drink of water, please?"

Slocum took the filled glass from the night table and poured some cool water down Sammy's parched throat.

Sammy said, "Everybody said I'd have to fight for what was mine, but I didn't. Maybe because I never had anything to fight for, I never believed in anything. I had my Aunt Meema and my Uncle Jake, my violin, and no worries. Once or twice a year, Aunt Meema would try to marry me off to some fat girl from the neighborhood. Maybe someday I would have been. I'd have had some children, made everyone proud, and worked myself into an early grave, dropping dead, God forbid, in the middle of Knickerbocker Avenue.

"Not a great life, but a safe one. But I've been doing a lot of thinking, and I have decided that safe can also be boring. And a boring life is like having one foot in the grave already. My cousin Hetzy says that some men die before their wives because they want to. No," Sammy went on. He looked at Emily and, even in his pain, he felt his heart leap at the sight of her. "I like this Texas. I like the people here— most of them, anyway. There's life here."

He studied Emily's shapely form, her curves and the swell of her firm breasts against the constraints of her dress. He said, "I fell in love with Texas." He took his hand in Emily's and squeezed it. "And I fell in love with a girl from Texas."

Emily blushed. Sammy said, "I like it here, I've decided. I want to stay and take what's mine."

Slocum shook his head. "It ain't safe, Sammy," he said. "You said it yourself. We're outnumbered, the odds are against us."

"The odds are against us today," Sammy said. "But odds can change under the right circumstances."

"I ain't sure I follow you, Sammy," Slocum said.

"Big problems call for bigger solutions," Sammy said. "And I think I've got one." He paused, trying to swallow so it didn't hurt. "I need to send a telegram back east."

"Your aunt and uncle can't help you out here, boy," Slocum said.

"It wasn't them I was thinking about," Sammy said.

At this point, there was an urgent knock on Miss Melody's front door. Doc Phipps had returned to tell Emily that her brother had been mortally wounded and some of Potter's men had her family virtually under siege at their ranch. Phipps had been allowed through the chain of Potter's hired guns to do what little he could for Billy Shields.

Emily started crying hysterically, and Melody went and took her upstairs to calm her down. Emily wanted to go to her family, but both Slocum and Doc Phipps wouldn't let her leave. "You'd be walking into a lot of flying lead," Phipps warned.

"I'm really starting to get mad," Sammy said. "About that telegram . . ."

16

Melnick the dry goods merchant crashed into a shelf loaded down with boxes of soap flakes he'd gotten from Henry the Goniff, a local thief who'd stolen a few cases of each off the back of a wagon on Livonia Avenue. Melnick, a chubby little man with beady eyes and no chin, bounced once off the shelf and plopped into a box full of whisk brooms, blood streaming from his mouth, from a hard left hook from Monk Westman.

"You lied to me, Melnick," Monk said. "I don't like it when people lie to me."

Melnick touched his hand to his mouth and looked at the blood, quaking with fear. Every week for the past two years he'd been paying Monk protection money, but he had been running behind in his payments, pleading bad business. Monk, out of the goodness of his heart, let Melnick slide for a few weeks. The weeks turned into a month, with Melnick always crying about how rotten business was.

Monk wanted his money. He rifled through the desk in Melnick's back room and found some very healthy deposit tickets from the Williamsburg Savings Bank. Business wasn't so bad after all. Now Monk really wanted his money. Plus, he was angry.

Melnick cowered in the corner of his store as Monk, surrounded by a half dozen of his boys, closed in around him.

"My hand to God, Monk," Melnick cried. "I was going to pay you Toisday."

Monk waved the deposit slips angrily and barked, "Three thousand you have in the bank, Melnick. You said things were bad, I trusted you. And you gave to me a spit in the face. Is this how you treat a friend?"

"I'll give you anything you want," Melnick said, his eyes wide in fear. "Just don't hit me again."

"I'm sorry, Melnick, but you got to be taught a lesson," Monk said, shaking his head. "Otherwise, word on the street would be, 'Monk Westman is a *putz*. Don't pay him.' "

Monk motioned to his boys. Gaspipe Rudnick, Dizzy Izzy Farkus, Ratface Cohen, Noodles Klein, and Mickey Feinstein pounced on Melnick, who vainly attempted to shield himself with his arms.

"Hurt him, but don't kill him," Monk said. "Dead, he can't pay *bupkus*."

Klepper the Schlepper hobbled into the store. He ran with a pronounced limp, the result of Monk's bullet in his knee. Klepper didn't hold a grudge, though, certainly not against someone like Monk Westman.

"Monk," he cried excitedly, waving an envelope. "This telegram just come for you, all the way from that Texas."

"Texas?" Monk said.

"Yeah," Klepper said breathlessly. He'd run all the way from the clubhouse. The Western Union messenger had refused to turn the telegram over to anyone but a Mr. Monk Westman. A few well-placed punches from Klepper to the messenger's face convinced him otherwise.

Monk grabbed the envelope, tore it open, and yanked out the message. He stared at it for a minute, then said, "Which one of you bagelheads knows from reading English?"

The boys stopped beating Melnick momentarily and looked at one another, shrugging.

"I know how," Melnick whimpered from the corner. His face was a bloody shambles.

Monk thrust the telegram at him.

"Oh, no," Melnick said. "I'll read it only if you stop from hitting on me."

"Read it," Monk snapped, "or I'll hit on you even worse."

Melnick took the telegram with a shaky hand and said, "Could someone maybe get my glasses? Next to the receipt pad by the cash register."

Klepper got the glasses and handed them to Melnick, who put them on and started reading the telegram—to himself.

"Out loud, *putz*," Monk snapped.

Melnick read it, slowly. It was from somebody named Samuel Kaminsky, from Roseville, Texas. He was in trouble by the sound of things. As Melnick continued reading, Monk's face went from pale white to beet red. He balled his fists in anger. The veins in his neck pulsed like baby snakes. Klepper half-expected to see steam spurt out Monk's ears. None of his boys, for that matter, had ever seen Monk so mad.

When Melnick finished reading the telegram, Monk blew his top. He put his fist through the wall, then grabbed a broom and sank his razor-sharp choppers into it until he bit it in half. His men shrank away, and Melnick covered his face with the telegram.

"His violin!" Monk thundered, stomping around the store in a purple rage, his eyes shiny black dots. "Those bastards smashed his violin."

"Maybe they heard him play it," Klepper the Schlepper suggested, then immediately regretted it. Monk loosened Klepper's front teeth with his fist.

"Nobody breaks Sammy's violin and lives to tell about it," Monk cried. He said to Ratface Cohen, "How much money we got, Ratface? How much?"

Cohen's mouth twitched. Monk was mad enough to chew nails. Cohen said, "A-about t-two thousand, Boss."

Monk turned to his boys. "Pack some stuff," he said, trying to keep his anger under lock and key. "We're going to this Texas."

"Texas?" Gaspipe Rudnick said. "Ain't that even farther than New Jersey?"

"I don't care if it's in China," Monk said. "We're going—and today."

Monk breathed heavily, his nostrils flaring as he got his anger under control. It was at this stage, his gang knew, that he was truly at his most dangerous, capable of just about anything that hurt and worse.

"I want to meet this Mr. Hiram Potter," Monk said.

Ben Tidley had been a conductor on any number of Texas railroad lines going on twenty years, had seen any number of plug-uglies from all points. But nothing quite prepared him for the motley band of six Easterners riding together in the last passenger car—scar-faced, pasty-looking boys, a cross between down-and-out Kansas City drummers and wild-eyed scalphunters from the Montana Territory.

They were killers, he knew, but not in any Texas gunslinging sense. They hadn't come this far west for the scenery.

Tidley punched the tickets that Monk Westman had handed him, looking at Monk's wretched mess of a face, chunks of which had been hacked off in ways Tidley did not care to imagine.

Tidley ventured some words. "Goin' to Killeen?" he asked.

Monk, staring straight ahead, said, "That's what it says on the tickets."

"Got business there, have you?" Tidley asked as pleasantly as possible.

Monk graced Tidley with his most menacing look, which wasn't difficult. "You talk too much," Monk said evenly, but his beady eyes told a different story: pain, torture, and possible dismemberment. "I think you should go away now," Monk said.

"Maybe I will at that," Tidley agreed, and moved on down the aisle.

Monk looked his boys over. Most of them were still in shock from their journey. None of them could have even remotely imagined what lay beyond the gardens of Hoboken, New Jersey, much less the dry, dusty west Texas plains. They'd live, Monk decided. Getting them this far, though, hadn't been easy. Most of them had wanted to bolt back to the safety of Williamsburg two hours out of the station, but Monk slapped, punched, and kicked them back into line.

"There's nuthin' here," Dizzy Izzy Farkus griped, looking at the endless hardscrabble landscape rolling by, as the train chugged along belching black smoke. "Where do you have lunch, take a bath, buy some smokes?"

"They got towns where you do that stuff," Monk snapped. He hadn't had a decent crap since they left Grand Central Station and was feeling irritable. The food out here was terrible—beans and rice and not a hunk of decent meat bigger than a man's toenail. They'd been *schlepping* on trains for what seemed like weeks, sleeping sitting up, sweating, and watching the world turn from green to brown out the windows.

But the journey was necessary, Monk knew. He had given Sammy his word to help, and everyone in New York City knew that Monk always kept his word. Now people in Texas would know as well, especially a man named Potter.

"Yup," Slocum said, watching Monk Westman and his boys climb off the wagon that had brought them to town. "They're New Yorkers, all right."

"Yes, they are," Sammy said.

Slocum studied Westman from across the street, where he and Sammy were waiting. Sammy was leaning on a crutch, his ankle still swollen. Aside from a lot of healing cuts and bruises, and a nose that was crooked where it once was straight, Sammy was more or less intact. He still had a bandage wrapped around his head.

Slocum had seen his share of scurvy, hard-looking men in his time, but few, outside of Yuma Prison, that looked as mean as Monk Westman and his gang. He said to Sammy, "Are you sure about this?"

"Rough times call for rough people, Mr. Slocum," Sammy said.

"I'm just wonderin' if the cure is worse than the disease," Slocum said.

"Try and keep an open mind," Sammy said, and made his way across Main Street toward the new arrivals. Slocum trailed behind.

Monk and his boys, Slocum saw, seemed genuinely happy to see Sammy again, save for his injuries. They took turns hugging him and shaking his hand and clapping him on the back. All the while, Potter's men, on horseback, were patrolling Main Street and flashing curious glances at Monk and company.

"And this is Mr. John Slocum," Sammy said, introducing him around. "The man who saved my life a couple of times."

Monk looked Slocum up and down, and decided to hold off judgment until he saw what the man was made of. Monk knew instinctively, though, that Slocum was one tough egg, one who didn't need to prove it to the world.

Monk shook his hand and said, "I owe you, pal."

Slocum said, "For what?"

"For keepin' my boy here breathin'," Monk said. "Means a lot to me."

Slocum shrugged. "Buy me a drink, we're even."

Sammy said, "You guys must be hungry."

"You ain't clickin' yer teeth," Gaspipe Rudnick said.

Ratface Cohen piped up. "Where ya get a pastrami sandwich around here? We ain't eaten decent since we left Brooklyn."

"Let's go to the cafe," Sammy said. "They're curing a brisket—"

Sammy had started to lead them to the cafe when Monk snapped at his gang, "Hold up there, rats. We got some business to attend to first."

"Aw, Monk, we're hungry," Dizzy Izzy said.

"Shaddup," Monk growled. He said to Slocum, "Where can I find this Potter *schmuck*?"

"Out to his ranch, probably," Slocum said.

"Then what are we wastin' time here for?" Monk said. "Let's get movin'."

On cue, his gang started pulling an assortment of weapons from their battered bags: blackjacks, knives, billy clubs, chains, razors, lead pipes, brass knuckles, and a variety of guns.

"Just hold on," Slocum said. "Those weapons may be okay for street fighting, but as you can see, streets are a little scarce in this part of the country. Besides," he added, "just what was it you had in mind?"

Monk said, "Potter broke Sammy's violin."

"He broke Sammy as well," Slocum said. "But that still don't answer my question."

Monk glared at Slocum and said, "What the hell you think I got in mind?"

"I already know," Slocum said, "and it ain't as easy as waltzin' up to him and killing him. And sure as hell not with weapons such as you got. Potter's got maybe twenty men workin' for him, and they shoot to kill. You got a plan, Mr. Westman, and I'll listen. But if you don't, you may do well to trust me for a spell."

Under ordinary circumstances, Monk would have killed any man for addressing him in the tone Slocum had, or even for not backing down. But for reasons he wasn't quite sure of, Monk sort of liked Slocum, might even see his way clear to trusting him.

Monk said, "Give me a reason why I should."

"There are two ways you can leave town," Slocum said. "In a carriage or in a coffin. Potter doesn't take prisoners."

"Neither do I," Monk said.

"We're outnumbered," Slocum said. "Vastly."

"My boys are tough, Slocum," Monk said. "The toughest in New York."

"So are Potter's," Slocum said, and motioned to a couple of Potter's hired guns standing in front of the saloon across the street.

Monk studied them for a minute and said, "No problem." He held his hand out and snapped at his boys, "Talk to me."

Dizzy Izzy slapped a hunk of lead pipe into Monk's hand. Monk strode confidently to the two men in front of the saloon. They watched him coming, their hands dropping to their holsters. Monk was upon them in seconds.

"You're with Potter?" Monk said to them. They towered over him by a good six or seven inches.

"Who the hell are you?" one of them said, spitting a stream of tobacco juice onto Monk's shoe.

"You spit on my shoe," Monk said. "Congratulations. You're on my bad side now."

It was over before Slocum could even blink. Monk whacked the man on the right over the head with the lead pipe, then in a flash jabbed it into the other one's belly. As the second man doubled over with a groan, Monk clunked him twice, opening a huge gash on the side of his head. Both men sagged to the street.

Monk came back, handed the bloody pipe to Dizzy Izzy, and said, "Clean this." He said to Slocum, "Whadda we do now?"

"We take this town back from Potter," Slocum said, duly impressed. "For now, get yourselves some rooms at the hotel, something to eat, and we'll talk later."

"Uh, Mr. Slocum," Sammy said timidly, "Mr. Potter took the hotel away from me."

"Then we gotta get it back, don't we?" Monk said.

"Come on, Esther," Wilson Gregory III said to the whorehouse madam. Happy Perkins was with him. "How much you take in today? Potter wants his money."

Esther Howard said nervously, "Maybe you better come back later, Wilson."

"What the hell for?" Gregory snapped. "We come to pick up Potter's earnings, so hand it over."

From the other side of the room, a voice said, "Your services ain't no longer necessary, ya bums."

Gregory and Happy Perkins saw a runt of a dude, no more than eighteen, sitting in a huge chair. He was dressed in a cheap city suit and wearing a derby.

"Who are you, stranger?" Gregory wanted to know.

"Name's Cohen, Albie Cohen, but some people call me Ratface. People I like." Ratface opened his coat. A tin deputy's badge was pinned on his coat pocket. "I'm whaddaya call a deppidy. That means I'm the law."

"What the hell are you talking about?" Gregory said, sounding disgusted. "Potter's the law in Roseville, not you. You're one of them peckerwood Yankee lowlifes Slocum and the Jew kid brought in, ain't you?"

"You know what your problem is?" Ratface said, standing. "You're not a very nice person."

"I'll show you how nice I am," Gregory said, charging at Ratface.

Ratface snapped his razor and slashed out even before Gregory reached him. Gregory didn't feel the first slice, which opened his left cheek, but he did feel the second—in one quick move Ratface slashed with the razor at the side of Gregory's head. Gregory felt a sting and then saw half an ear—his—pinched between Ratface's thumb and forefinger.

Gregory slapped his hand to the side of his head. There was shredded, ragged flesh where his ear had been.

"So tell me how nice you are," Ratface said. "I'm all ear."

Wilson Gregory III was quite a sight. Blood streamed down his face from the gash in his cheek, and more blood trickled between his fingers as he stared dumbly at his freshly severed ear. He howled in pain.

"Sweet Jesus," Happy Perkins muttered.

"From that I wouldn't know," Ratface Cohen said to him. "Take your friend and get the hell outta here or there's more where this came from." He tossed the severed ear to Perkins, who caught it and then wished he hadn't. Not knowing what else to do, he stuffed it into Gregory's shirt pocket and helped his wounded friend out the door.

"I want you both outta town—by Sunday," Ratface snarled.

"I think you mean by sundown," Perkins called back.

"Even better," Ratface replied. He turned to Esther Howard, who looked paler than warm milk, even under ten coats of face paint, and said, "Anyone else comes around, you let me know."

"I can do that," Esther said, nodding, images of bloody ears in her mind.

"Gimme a seltzer," Dizzy Izzy Farkus said to the bartender.

"A what?" the bartender said, puzzled.

"Seltzer, fizz water," Dizzy Izzy said. "A glass two cents of plain." Down at the end of the bar, two of Potter's men eyeballed the stranger, one of the bunch who'd arrived yesterday. "What, you ain't got any?" Dizzy Izzy said.

"He don't look so tough," one of the men at the end of the bar said to his friend.

"I serve hard whiskey and beer," the bartender shot back. "You want something else, you can—"

Dizzy Izzy smiled and grabbed the bartender by the collar. He slammed the barkeep's face down onto the bar a couple of times and could hear the crunch of cartilage and bone. Dizzy Izzy knew the bartender was working for Potter; the saloon was one of the businesses Potter had stolen from Sammy.

"You was saying?" the other man said to his friend.

"I ast you a question," Dizzy Izzy said to the bartender.

The bartender snorted and sputtered as blood gushed from his smashed nose. Dizzy Izzy still held firm to the man's collar.

"Potter ain't a-gonna like this," said the first man at the end of the bar. He strode over to Dizzy Izzy and said, "You ain't what I'd call polite, friend."

Dizzy Izzy pushed the bartender away and spun around. He saw a tall, thin man dressed like the rest of these Texas shitkickers. The man had two Colt six-shooters tucked into a crazy belt these cowboys called holsters.

"Who the hell are you?" Dizzy Izzy asked, then added, "and why are you lettin' your shadow fall all over me?"

"Name's Crispin," the man said, "and I'll throw my shaddy anywhere I want in *my* town."

"*Oy,* so this is *your* town, is it?" Dizzy Izzy wanted to know. This Crispin guy towered a foot over him, probably outweighed him by thirty pounds. "Let me tell you something, Mr. Fancy-Pants big Texas man. I wouldn't let my dog live in this shitbox town of yours, if I had a dog. Whaddaya think of that?"

"This," Crispin snapped, and reached for his Colt.

Dizzy Izzy, like lightning, grabbed a handful of Crispin's crotch in a vice-like grip and squeezed with all his might. It wasn't too difficult—these Texas men liked tight-fitting jeans, which made Dizzy Izzy's job easier.

Crispin yelped in pain, but not for long. With his free hand, Dizzy Izzy whipped a knife, seemingly from out of nowhere, and buried it deep in Crispin's heart. Crispin's face registered shock as Dizzy Izzy released him and the cowboy crumpled to the floor.

It all happened so fast that Crispin's buddy barely had time to react. He spun, drawing his pistol, and fired off a shot at Dizzy Izzy, unaware that the Yankee had already thrown his knife, and that the shot barely winged him.

When Crispin's buddy saw Dizzy Izzy fall to the floor, he holstered his gun and turned back to the bar.

"Mess with me," he grumbled, and poured himself a drink. He looked in the mirror over the bar and saw his reflection. The Yankee's knife was firmly imbedded in his belly. The pain followed.

He saw Dizzy Izzy rise up off the floor, dusting off his jacket, then walk over to him.

"Explain this one to your goilfriend," Dizzy Izzy said, and grabbed the hilt of the knife. He gave it a twist. Crispin's friend groaned. He could feel the life draining out of him.

"Once a sucker, always a sucker," Dizzy Izzy muttered, then gave the knife another twist for good luck, and yanked it out. Still holding him, Dizzy Izzy wiped his bloody knife on the man's shirt, then pushed him away. The man dropped like a sack of fish.

Dizzy Izzy yelled to everyone in the saloon, "From now on, this dump belongs to Sammy Kaminsky. Anyone what feels different should come talk with me."

He turned to the bar. The bartender, holding a bloody rag to his nose, had true fear in his eyes.

"Now," Dizzy Izzy said calmly. "What about my seltzer?"

By five o'clock, Monk and his minions had taken back Roseville.

They were having dinner in the cafe, fried chicken and mashed potatoes. Monk was at the head of the table, Sammy next to him, looking slightly dazed.

Slocum sat at the other end of the table. He was off his food and instead chewed a toothpick. He watched Sammy's New York friends stuffing themselves, like a band of bloodthirsty Comanche after a murder raid. Yes, Slocum admitted to himself, Monk and his gang had been victorious, taking Roseville back from Potter in a day and a half. But at what cost? Two dead men, and several disfigured for life.

"Whassamatter, Slocum?" Monk said. "Ain't hungry?"

"Nope," Slocum answered. "Killin' ruins my appetite."

Monk's eyes narrowed. He sensed trouble. "Whaddaya talking about, tall man? We did good today. Sure, some mugs hadda die, but that's the price of defendin' your turf."

"They were still people, even if they did work for Potter," Slocum said. "We could have handled them some other way—"

"The hell we could," Monk snapped, biting into a chicken leg. "Most times, the threat of killing is enough to keep the suckers in line, but this wasn't one of 'em. You got to put fear into their hearts, and sometimes you got to do it quick. If that means killin', then so be it." He put his arm around Sammy's shoulder. "What, you think this Potter sap wouldn't kill my Sammy here?"

Sammy looked uncomfortable.

Slocum said, "He could have, a couple of times. But he didn't."

"Sometimes I wonder whose side yer on," Monk said.

"I used to know," Slocum said. "I ain't so sure as of now."

"You know what your trouble is, John Slocum?" Monk said. "You're just mad 'cause you needed help, my brand of help. You couldn't handle this one alone, and it pissed you off." A hint of a grin crossed Monk's lips. "Don't be so hard on yourself, tall man. Nobody coulda done more than you did. You kept my boy alive long enough so's I could get here."

"What now?" Slocum said. "You put me out to pasture?"

"Don't be a *schmuck*," Monk said. "We need you still, more than ever. Now that tomorrow we're gonna attack Potter's place."

"You're what?" Slocum asked, not sure he'd heard right.

"That's right," Monk repeated. "Tomorrow we find Potter and kill him."

"That's crazy," Slocum snapped, jumping up. "Potter'll have twenty men guarding him at his ranch, and let me tell you, friend, that as sure as I'm standing here, Eustace Potter is madder than a hive of honeybees in a hailstorm.

You killed two of his boys today, and he won't cotton to that. It's war, Monk, all-out war, and he won't just be settin' on his ass waitin' fancy-like so's you can waltz through his front door."

"Yes, he will," Monk said. "He'll never be expecting us to come to him. That's why we got to. Anyone can win a war on their own turf, Slocum. The trick is to bring the war to the enemy, on *his* turf."

"A lot of people will die, Monk," Slocum said. "Unless you got a plan. And it better be a damn good one."

"Me and my boys," Monk said, "we got some tricks for Potter and his gang of cow-kissing copperhorns."

"I think he means tinhorns," Sammy said. He stood. "Can I be excused?"

"What for? Where you goin'?" Monk said.

Sammy cleared his throat nervously and stammered, "Uh, I have an appointment."

"With who?"

"With a very fine young lady, Monk," Slocum said. "For Christ's sake, cut him some slack."

"Awright," Monk said. "Go see your woman. Don't do nuthin' I wouldn't do." He chortled. "Ratface, go with him, just in case."

"It's really not that far, just over to Miss Melody's house," Sammy said. Before anyone could respond, he made a hasty exit. As he was going out, he heard Monk say, "Ya know, a woman wouldn't go down bad right about now. How many whores they got over at that cathouse?"

Sammy walked down Main Street toward Miss Melody's house. It was dusk, the Texas sun setting in all its orange glory. Sammy had never seen so much sky in one place as in Texas. It was very impressive.

As he strode down the plank sidewalk, Luke Price stepped out from the alley and faced Sammy, who stopped dead in his tracks.

"Ung," Sammy said, his bowels turning into water. He spun on the heels of his shoes to start walking in the opposite direction. Facing him now was Happy Perkins. Both men started walking toward Sammy, who hastily crossed the street. Al Bridge stepped out from behind a post in front of the mercantile.

Bridge moved toward Sammy, who opened his mouth to call out. He felt something pointy pressed against his spine. Something like the barrel of a gun.

Sammy started to turn and saw from the corner of his eye that Luke Price was also holding a gun on him.

"Move another muscle and I'll blow your guts out," Price hissed.

Al Bridge and Happy Perkins surrounded Sammy. He felt light in the head. This was going to be very bad.

"You're coming with us," Bridge said. "One word and you're dead."

"So I've been told," Sammy murmured.

He felt something crash down on his head. He was unconscious even before the blood started seeping from his skull.

17

"Yeah," Monk was saying. "Nothing beats a bad meal better than a bad woman." He stood and stretched as his associates lit up cigars and relaxed. "Which way to the closest house of ill refute?"

"Go left out the door, cop a walk, and you'll see a joint what's got a lot of horses tied up outside," Noodles Klein said.

"You should do me a favor, Noodles," Monk said. "Go over there and pick out the best girl for me. You know how I like 'em. *Zaftig,* big and bouncy with a nice round *tuchas.*"

"Right away, Boss," Noodles Klein said, and clamped down on his cigar. He jammed his cap on his head and went to the door.

Before Klein was even halfway through, a shot rang out. Klein flew backward through the door and crashed into a table. There was a huge hole where his left eye had been. The cigar was still clenched between his teeth, even now, in death.

More shots exploded, shattering the window glass. Slocum, Monk, and the others dove to the floor as more shots pinged into the cafe.

"So much for bringing the war to them," Slocum said.

"Bastards," Monk bellowed.

"He's dead, Boss," Ratface cried, examining their fallen comrade. "For this we'll make them pay!"

"Who's packin' a gun?" Slocum barked.

"I am," Monk said.

"I got," Dizzy Izzy said.

On all fours, they scrambled over to the shattered windows. Slocum peered out. He saw at least a dozen men shooting at the cafe. They were hidden behind wagons and woodpiles and in rooms in the hotel across the street. Potter had them pinned down pretty damn nicely.

Monk and Dizzy Izzy were firing blindly out the window. Monk called out, "There a back door to this place?"

"Yeah," Slocum responded. "Opens up into the alley. But my guess is they got that covered, too."

"You might be right," Monk said. "Gaspipe, go see."

Gaspipe Rudnick suddenly looked panic-stricken. "What if there is and they got guns?"

"Then they'll probably shoot at you," Monk said. "If you don't go, *I'll* shoot at you."

Gaspipe crawled across the floor and under tables. "Texas he takes us," he grumbled as he wormed his way into the kitchen. "He couldn't take us someplace nice, like Paris or Balti-more. No, he takes us to this stinky Texas."

Huddled in the corner of the kitchen were Amelia, the cockeyed old lady who served the food, and Rosita, a rotund Mexican who cooked it. They were whimpering.

"Don't hurt us," Amelia sobbed. "If this is about the glass in the stew the other day—"

"Shut up," Gaspipe snapped. "I ain't the one who's shootin' at you. It's that rat bastard Potter."

Gaspipe started to go to the kitchen door and stopped abruptly. He turned to the two women cowering in the corner and said to Rosita, "Take a look outside, chubby, and tell me if you see somethin'."

Rosita started crying and babbling in Mexican. Gaspipe

grabbed her by her flabby arm and shoved her to the door.

"Now open it and look out and tell me what you see," Gaspipe said, standing directly behind her.

Rosita did as she was told. Three shots rang out. She screamed and pulled her head back inside. She lost her balance and fell backward—on top of Gaspipe, knocking the wind out of his lungs.

Rosita was well on her way to hysteria, flailing her meaty arms and legs as Gaspipe attempted to dislodge himself from under her bulk.

"Get offa me, you big cow," Gaspipe squealed, pushing her off. "They got the alley covered, too, Monk," he called out.

"What now, Boss?" Ratface asked. "This is even worse than when the Hudson Street Dusters caught us on the waterfront."

"How *did* we get out of that one?" Monk asked hopefully.

"We dived into the river," Ratface said.

"Shit," Monk said.

Sizzling lead continued pounding into the cafe's walls and floorboards. Then the shooting stopped abruptly and a deep voice boomed out from across the street, "Hold your fire, Slocum." It was unmistakably Potter's voice. "We got your boy over here."

Slocum and Monk looked out. In the middle of Main Street, Sammy, semiconscious, was held up by Luke Price and Happy Perkins. Each was holding a six-shooter on him.

"Son of a bitch," Slocum hissed. "This don't look promising."

"Throw out your guns," Potter barked, "and then I want you and them Eastern peckerwoods to come out real slow-like. Else I'll put a bullet in your boy's head."

"I don't know what a peckerwood is, but I hate it already," Monk said angrily.

"I can take the one on the left," he said, aiming at Luke Price. "You get the one on—"

"No!" Slocum snapped. "Let me handle this."

He tossed his gun through the window and yelled, "All right, Potter. I'm comin' out. Just don't shoot the kid."

Slocum kicked open the cafe door and walked out, hands held high. His luck was holding. Nobody shot at him.

"I gave him the chance to leave town while he was still breathin'," Potter said. "An' he runs in a passel of pissant Yankees to bluff me."

Inside the cafe, Monk asked Ratface Cohen angrily, "What's a pissant?"

"I don't know," Ratface said, "but it don't sound nice."

Potter continued, "My patience is wearin' thin, Slocum. Real thin."

"Give me the kid," Slocum said. "I'll put him on the train my own self. His friends, too."

"It's too late, Slocum," Potter yelled. "Y'all pushed me too far. You can have your boy—dead! Let him have it, boys."

Perkins and Luke Price shoved Sammy to the ground and aimed at his head.

"No, Potter!" Slocum cried. "We'll—"

Two shots exploded. Slocum was sure Sammy was dead. The shots, though, seemed to have come from somewhere else. Perkins crumpled dead on the street. Luke Price darted back to the safety of the hotel, and made it.

Slocum didn't know who had fired the shots, and didn't much care. He dashed over to Sammy and slung him over his shoulder. The shooting began anew, and bullets whizzed by Slocum's head as he staggered back to the cafe.

Ten feet from the door, he felt something hot rip through his left calf. He collapsed, sending both himself and Sammy sprawling on the plank sidewalk, ten feet from the cafe door. Monk and Ratface Cohen appeared, grabbing Slocum and Sammy and pulling them inside. Somebody was shooting back at Potter and his men.

"You got some friends you don't know about?" Monk

said, back at the window and firing again. He was down to his last two bullets.

"Guess I do," Slocum said, white-hot pain burning through his leg. He grabbed a steak knife from the floor and ripped his jeans up the side. The bullet had fortunately only grazed him, but it was a messy graze. He wrapped a few napkins around his calf. It would do for the time being.

"I'm almost dry," Dizzy Izzy said. "Anyone got bullets?"

"No," Monk said. "We need bullets," he said to Slocum.

"What the hell you want me to do?" Slocum said, tying off the makeshift bandage. "Why don't you throw some of Rosita's biscuits at them? They're almost as deadly as bullets."

"Everybody's a smarthead," Monk grumbled.

"Sammy," Mickey Feinstein said, slapping Sammy to bring him around. "Speak to me, kid. Say a few syllables."

Sammy's eyes fluttered open. "Emily?" he said weakly. "Is that you?"

"C'mon, kid," Feinstein said, slapping him gently again. "Wake up already."

Sammy suddenly remembered where he was. He groaned, the pain in his head excrutiating.

"You okay, kid?" Feinstein asked.

Sammy groaned again and said, "Maybe I'll die and this will all be over."

Slocum picked up a gun and aimed out the window, about to squeeze off a shot at one of Potter's men, who was reloading behind a woodpile, his head within view. Before he could fire, Slocum heard another shot and saw the man's head snap back like a bottle top, as he disappeared from view.

"If we could just get to the hotel," Monk said. "All our weapons are stashed there."

"Right where Potter's men can find them," Slocum said.

"I ain't no stupe," Monk snapped. "I hid 'em."

"Where?" Slocum said.

"Third-floor broom closet, under a pile of rags," Monk said.

"One of us has to make a run for it, spread the fight out," Slocum said. "Potter will set fire to this side of Main Street to smoke us out if he has to. Once he does, we're all cooked. Here's what we do. I'll make a dash out the front; you cover me. Between you and our new friends, I can make it to the hotel—"

"Forget it, Slocum," Monk said. "You won't get six inches with that leg. I know how to dodge bullets. Shit, I do it every day back in Brooklyn."

Monk checked the chamber on his gun. He had two bullets left.

"Gaspipe, you still there?" he hollered.

"I'm here, Boss," Gaspipe called from the kitchen.

"Grab a mop and wait for me."

Monk crawled into the kitchen through the swinging door. Gaspipe was waiting, clutching a mop. Amelia and Rosita were still huddled in the corner.

"With the mop, I want you should open the door," Monk told Gaspipe.

Gaspipe nodded. He knew this move. He opened the alley door a crack, then pushed it all the way with the head of the mop. A second later, two rifle shots boomed and took out a chunk of the door. At that exact moment, Monk leapt out into the alley.

He was facing two men who were trying to reload their double-barreled shotguns. Monk aimed at one, fired, then aimed at the other and fired. Both men crumpled to the ground.

Monk turned and dashed down the alley, away from Main Street. Gaspipe Rudnick was right behind him. They came out behind the blacksmith's, then crept along the backs of the buildings on the south side of Main Street, toward the edge of town.

They made their way behind the bank. This was more

like it, Monk mused. Slithering around buildings and creeping around dark alleyways was more his style.

A gunshot roared in his ears and kicked up the soil six inches from his foot in mid-step.

"Another inch and I'll blow your butt off," came a voice, definitely female, above them.

Monk and Gaspipe looked up to the roof of the bank. Two women were aiming rifles at them: Miss Melody and Miss Emily. Monk recognized them.

"Just what the hell you think you're doin'?" he wanted to know.

"Pulling your fat out of the fire," Miss Melody replied. "That's what." She turned, cocked her Winchester, and squeezed off another shot at the enemy. "What are you doing here?"

Monk and Gaspipe were momentarily stunned at the highly unusual sight of two dames—and two good-looking dames at that—firing rifles that were almost as big as they were. Finally Monk said, "We're runnin' outta bullets. Where can I get more?"

Melody and Emily ignored Monk for a moment, crouching low and reloading, then firing anew at the hotel. Melody said, "Where does anybody get bullets? Over to the mercantile."

"What's a mercantile and where do I find it?" Monk snapped.

"Across the street," Melody said. "But you'll never make it."

"I will if you cover me," Monk said, and darted into the adjoining alley. Melody opened her mouth to protest, but Monk was already gone, having vanished like a shadow.

"Is he crazy?" Emily cried, watching as Monk sprinted out into the middle of Main Street, dodging bullets that kicked up puffs of dust at his feet.

"To speak the truth," Gaspipe said, peering out onto Main Street from behind the bakery, "the answer is a definite yes."

"He'll never make it," Melody said.

"Don't bet against it," Gaspipe said.

Melody and Emily continued firing at the hotel. Potter's men were pouring lead at Monk, who ducked and dodged the firestorm, zigzagging across Main Street like a spider in a sizzling skillet.

Inside the cafe, Slocum and the others watched in stunned amazement at Monk's almost balletic dance, successfully missing every bullet fired by a dozen men. Slocum had never seen anything like it.

"Shit, can that bastard move," he said, impressed.

"You ain't just clickin' yer teeth," Dizzy Izzy Farkus responded.

"God*damn*," Potter said, watching Monk as he miraculously made it across Main Street. The ugly, scarred man was a minion of the devil. No man could have that much hot lead blasted at him and live to tell about it. It slowly dawned on Potter, and his men, that they'd all stopped firing to watch Monk's city-bred instincts take control over his lithe body. Then they remembered that Monk was the enemy and started blasting away once more.

Too late. Monk dove through the plate glass mercantile window, exploding it into hundreds of shards.

Potter grinned. He had anticipated something like this happening, and had planted some insurance inside the place.

Monk was vaguely aware that he had some company inside the mercantile, even as he hurtled through the window. He rolled himself into a ball and careened into a table laden with a new shipment of expensive china from St. Louis. Plates and saucers and teacups flew everywhere. Monk bounced off the table, rolled, and came up on his feet.

He pivoted, yanking a shiv from his pocket, and flung it in the direction of a shadow emerging from behind a rack of glass bottles. Monk heard a painful grunt, then saw one of Potter's men drop his gun, then die on his feet.

Monk pulled the knife from the man's gut. He stepped neatly over the dead body into the storeroom. "Nice try, asshole," Monk said to the inert form sprawled on the sawdust-covered floor.

Inside the storeroom were guns and more guns, a cache of weapons unlike any Monk had ever eyeballed—pistols, repeating rifles, all the latest fashions from Remington and Smith & Wesson. These Texas people did love their guns.

Monk liked guns, too. He decided to try a few on for size.

At this point, only the unknown shooters from the rooftop down the street were keeping Slocum and the others alive. Slocum had fired his last shot, as had Dizzy Izzy. They huddled in various places around the cafe, behind the wooden tables. Shots pinged around them.

Slocum had seen Monk crash through the mercantile window, and was duly impressed, though there was always that thin line between bravery and stupidity. Monk had come in just above it.

Sammy was finally coming around. Ratface Cohen helped him along by pouring a pitcher of water onto his face. Sammy immediately sat up, fully conscious, and banged his head against an overturned table. He went back to sleep again.

"Shit," Cohen muttered, and slapped Sammy's face until he came to again.

"Aunt Meema?" Sammy asked, his eyes glazed over like the top of a honeycake.

"No, kid," Ratface said, cradling Sammy. "You're here, in Texas. Don't you remember?"

"Texas," Sammy muttered, his mind thousands of miles away. "I know this Texas."

Ratface slapped Sammy's cheek gently. "C'mon, kid, it's me, Ratface. Whaddaya say?"

"Tell me a story," Sammy said dreamily.

"A story?" Ratface said indignantly.

"Tell me the one about the mean golem and the greedy village merchant who makes the deal with him."

"I ain't never heard that story before," Ratface said.

"You remember," Sammy said, grinning like a drunken idiot. "The golem is God's dark messenger, whenever God is mad at someone. And God is mad because the merchant wants more money, and He sends the golem to teach the merchant a lesson."

"Yeah?" Ratface said, interested now. "What's that golem guy do to the merchant?"

"He takes the merchant's firstborn male child," Sammy said, trying to remember.

"What the hell's he do that for?" Ratface asked, astonished. "That ain't nice."

"It's because the merchant is greedy and cares more about money than he does about love or life," Sammy said, fully conscious now. "Or something like that."

"That's stupid," Ratface snapped, pushing Sammy away in disgust. He said angrily, "The merchant's just tryin' to make a buck, for God's sake. What the hell's wrong with that?"

"I was just—" Sammy started.

"Hey, I know God's good and all that stuff," Ratface ranted, "but He got no right stickin' His nose into someone's business. And the hell with that golem guy, too. You send him around to see me, he'll sing a different tune. You got that?"

"It's just a story," Sammy said, sitting up. He felt faint for a moment, until the blood in his head went back to where it was supposed to be. His head hurt and no mistake.

"It's stupid," Ratface said, and let it go at that as bullets slammed into the wooden floor all around them.

"Well, shit on a stick." They all heard Slocum utter this, admiration in his tone. Slocum was perched by the window, looking out at something.

Noodles grabbed Sammy and dragged him over to the window. Looking out, they saw a sight that made them gasp in awe.

Monk was diving out of the mercantile and behind the safety of a horse trough. He was wielding two six-shooters, firing in the direction of the hotel with both barrels.

"Die, you bastards!" he bellowed, blasting away.

Bandoliers crisscrossed Monk's chest. He was wearing a ten-gallon hat, three gallons too small, bending his one good ear incongruously. A burlap sack full of rifles was slung over his shoulder. His eyes were blacker than the depths of hell, his face contorted into a mask of fury. He jumped up and started darting back across Main Street. For the first few moments his luck held; the bullets from Potter's hired guns merely kicked up dust several feet away from him. Monk continued shooting back until, fifteen feet away from the cafe, he took a hunk of lead in the left shoulder. Slocum saw Monk mouth the word "shit" and watched as he flew backward on his ass, his shoulder spurting blood.

Praying that their unseen friends on the rooftop would cover him, Slocum burst from the door of the cafe and limped to Monk. Shots rang out and whizzed by Slocum's ears like ravenous mosquitoes. He grabbed Monk under the arms and dragged him back to the cafe, Monk still firing away with his good arm.

"Nothing personal, Monk," Slocum muttered as he dragged the fallen gang leader toward the safety of the cafe, "but you're beginning to get on my nerves."

"I ain't exactly in love with you neither," Monk replied, firing away.

Slocum managed to drag Monk back inside the cafe. He opened the door, which was riddled with bullet holes, pulled Monk inside, then kicked the door shut.

Monk said, "I owe you, Slocum."

"You owe me nothing," Slocum responded.

Bleeding like a stuck pig, Monk started yanking guns from the burlap sack and tossing them at his boys, who caught them expertly, like seasoned war veterans. They crept back to the cafe windows and started fighting back.

Monk pulled one last Colt .44 from the burlap bag and handed it to Sammy.

"This one's for you kid. You get me?"

Sammy looked down at the gun in his hands. Guns brought nothing but misery, he had decided. "I—"

"This is war, Sammy," Monk said. "You fight or you die."

Sammy looked frantically over at Slocum, who met his anguished gaze.

"He's right," Slocum said, somewhat grudgingly.

Monk handed Slocum a Winchester rifle. Slocum graciously accepted it.

Monk tossed some shells at Slocum and said, "Do your best, tall man."

"I will," Slocum said, and loaded his weapon. He added, "Do something about that shoulder."

"I already did," Monk said. "I forgot about it. Bullet only took off a small piece. It ain't nuthin'."

"Suit yourself," Slocum said, then turned and fired out the window. Slocum's butt was still burning at the sight of Monk's skillful moves. He ruefully remembered the time when he was still capable of such tricks.

Gaspipe burst through the kitchen door and dove to the floor. He said excitedly, "It's the broads, them pretty broads. They're on the roof of the bank."

"What broads?" Slocum asked, grabbing a tablecloth and ripping off a chunk, which he used to press against Monk's shoulder wound.

"That's right, tall man," Monk said, "Your lady friend, Miss Melody. And that girl Sammy's got a stiff *schlong* for, that Miss Emily. They're backing us up."

"Those crazy fools," Slocum said, scrambling to his feet and heading for the back door. Sammy, clutching the Colt, was right behind him.

18

Slocum and Sammy crept along the back of Main Street, darting past alleyways, toward the bank. Slocum tried to ignore the fiery pain in his leg, but the pain threatened to win. Sammy had never been so scared in his life, but he felt a strange sort of exhilaration. There was something exciting about the sounds of guns barking all over town, though barely.

They were maybe fifty yards away from the bank. Even from here, they could see the two women still firing from the roof.

"God-*damn,*" Slocum muttered.

Sammy felt a pang of love for Miss Emily as he watched her squeeze off a shot.

The pang went from love to horror as she took a bullet and fell over backward. Miss Melody screamed and bent to help her. The firing from inside the cafe continued.

"Bastards!" Sammy bellowed, and started to charge into the alley. Before he got two inches, Slocum grabbed him by the collar and yanked him back. He slammed Sammy up against the wall and slapped him hard in the face.

"Not a smart move, boy," Slocum said.

"Emily—" Sammy blurted.

Slocum nodded. "We need to go to her."

They made their way to the back of the bank. They opened the window and climbed inside. In the back room a ladder led up to the roof. A dead body, one of Potter's men, lay on the floor a foot from the ladder. Either Melody or Emily had plugged the intruder. How many surprises, Slocum wondered, did this one day have in store? Slocum and Sammy climbed, and Slocum pushed the hatch open. Miss Melody was crouching low beside Miss Emily.

Emily's right arm was covered with blood. Sammy started to rush to her, but Slocum grabbed him by the seat of his pants.

"Crawl, don't run, Sammy," he said.

They crawled across the rooftop. Sammy went to Emily and took her hand.

Shock was setting in quickly, but she still smiled at the sight of her new man.

"Hello, Sammy," she said weakly.

"Hello, Emily," he said, fighting back tears.

Slocum said to Melody, "Don't think I need to tell you how unhappy I am about you two getting mixed up in this."

"Save it, John," Melody said. "You needed our help."

This was true. Slocum said, "If we ever get out of this alive, I'm taking you over my knee and slapping your bottom till you beg me to stop."

"That sounds very interesting," Melody said, mopping the blood from Emily's wound.

Slocum examined Emily. The wound itself wasn't necessarily fatal—the loss of blood, however, could prove otherwise.

"We've got to get her out of here," Slocum said. "I'll keep Potter and his boys busy; you and Sammy get her downstairs."

As they carried Emily toward the hatch, Slocum crawled to the edge of the roof and started firing. That's when he saw the two riders galloping down Main Street from the west, and riding hard.

As they approached, Slocum saw that both riders were clutching sticks of dynamite, and those sticks were lit, the fuses sizzling. Slocum had little doubt where they were headed.

As they passed in front of the bank, Slocum aimed and fired. The rider on the outside pitched forward in the saddle and tumbled to the street, his dynamite rolling toward the mercantile.

One of Potter's men dashed out from behind a horse trough and grabbed the bundle. The fuse was maybe a third of an inch from the end. The man was about to throw it across the street when Slocum put a bullet in his belly. He fell to the street, still clutching the dynamite. A second later a deafening roar filled the air, followed by a brilliant flash of light. Blood, dirt, and bone fragments splattered everywhere.

The second rider, meanwhile, rode up adjacent to the cafe and pitched the dynamite at the shattered window as hard as he could, then rode off.

He scored a direct hit. The lethal bundle sailed neatly through the window. Inside the cafe, Monk and his boys watched the sparkling fuse fizzle into the gates of hell.

"Run away!" Monk bellowed, and the Westman Gang scrambled toward the kitchen en masse. Two seconds later a roar pierced the afternoon and the entire front wall of the cafe disintegrated, blowing outward into the street. Monk and his boys were all knocked silly.

The thing was, Ratface discovered just as the dynamite exploded, Monk was nowhere to be seen.

Eustace Potter ran upstairs to the third floor of the hotel and kicked open the door to one of the rooms that faced Main Street. He looked out the window and smiled at what he saw.

The front of the cafe no longer existed; a huge, smoking hole now appeared, big enough for an elephant to amble through. Potter smiled. His boys had done good. There was no movement from inside the cafe. Good, Potter thought.

All that remained was that pain-in-the-butt John Slocum, who was crouched low on the roof of the bank. Slocum's attention, Potter could see, was directed elsewhere. Potter aimed, and had a clear shot at Slocum's head.

Before he could fire, he felt the barrel of a gun prod the back of his head.

"Fire that gun and you'll never play the violin again," Potter heard a voice behind him utter. He relaxed his finger on the trigger of his Sharps and turned his head around slowly.

That Yankee scum, the one everyone called Monk, was leering at him.

"How the hell did you—" Potter started.

"Get here?" Monk finished. "Never turn yer back on a New Yorker." He smiled again. The effect, to Potter, was like a grinning skull. This was the first time he'd actually seen Monk up close. He was not a feast for the eyes. Parts of his face were ripped, scarred, or missing altogether. Potter felt his heart flutter in fear. This man meant business.

"Now, stand up real slow, and drop that cannon you're holdin'," Monk said. Potter did, and the Sharps clattered to the floor. He turned to face Monk.

"You're a dead man," Potter said through clenched teeth. "You're deader than dead."

Monk sighed tiredly. "I'm makin' chocolate in my drawers, pal, I'm so scared," he said. "We're goin' now. There's some things we gotta do."

"Goin' where?" Potter asked, as Monk nudged him forward.

"None of your damn business," Monk said.

Sammy and Miss Melody gently placed Emily down on a wooden table. They covered her with some aprons Melody grabbed off a shelf.

"She needs Doc Phipps," Melody said. "Looks like the bullet in her shoulder is in pretty deep. Too deep."

Emily was out cold. Her face was whiter than flour.

"Emily," Sammy said, his voice cracking as he looked down at her. Her getting shot was his fault, he was sure; just as his coming to Roseville had tilted the balance of things for the worse. A lot of people were dead because of him. "I'm sorry, Emily. If I only—"

"I know what you're thinking, Sammy," Miss Melody said to him. "None of this was your fault. It's Potter and his greed that did it. You only wanted what was yours. In Texas, a man has to fight sometimes for it."

Sammy looked at her, his eyes wider than saucers. Melody saw something in them she'd not seen before— rage, and a little hate as well.

"This ends now," Sammy said. "Now."

He turned, the Colt shoved into his pocket, and started walking toward the front of the bank. Melody ran up to him and grabbed his arm before he could go out the front door.

"Sammy, are you crazy?" she asked. "You won't get two feet before they blast you."

"Then let them," Sammy said. "Maybe then all the killing will stop."

"Sammy—" Melody started. Her words were cut off by the sounds of church bells booming through Roseville. And it wasn't Sunday morning.

At the east end of Main Street was the Roseville Baptist Church. All eyes turned to see Monk swinging back and forth on the bell rope atop the steeple. Potter was standing on the ledge, with one end of a rope around his neck, the other end tied to the clapper, with maybe three feet of slack. One move off the steeple and Potter's neck would stretch like warm taffy. Monk had taken the added precaution of binding Potter's hands behind his back.

"Throw out your guns," Monk yelled, once the bell had stopped clanging. He stood behind Potter. "Come out slow. Screw with me and I give your boss a push he'll never forget."

"That son of a bitch," Slocum said to himself. How the

hell had Monk got from the cafe to the hotel? The man continued to amaze Slocum. Slocum hated him more than ever, but he hated him with a great deal of respect.

"You hear me?" Monk roared. "I don't see no guns bein' throwed out."

For a few moments, it was a stalemate. No shots were fired, but neither were any guns tossed out. Monk plucked a knife from his pocket and poked it into Potter's meaty ass. Potter howled.

"Maybe you better tell 'em," Monk said.

"Do what he says, you peckerwoods!" Potter wailed.

One by one, guns were tossed out, until a small arsenal littered Main Street.

"Tell 'em to come out with their hands up," Monk said to Potter. He was clutching Potter's belt.

"Get your miserable asses out there," Potter called.

Potter's men trickled slowly out onto the street, hands held high.

"Slocum," Monk cried. "You still in one piece, Slocum?"

"I'm here," Slocum called back from the bank roof.

"Do me a favor," Monk called. "Round up those clowns and slap their asses in your jail."

It was, Slocum mused, as good a plan as any. He scampered back to the hatch and was climbing down the ladder when he heard Melody cry out, "No, Sammy, don't!"

Sammy drew his Colt and walked out into the middle of Main Street. In front of the hotel, Luke Price stood next to Al Bridge. Their arms were raised, but Sammy saw hate in their eyes.

Sammy walked up to Luke Price and the rest of Potter's toadies.

Sammy said, "Which one of you rat bastards shot Miss Emily?"

Luke Price spit into the street. He said, "Was me. What're you a-gonna do about it, you gutless puke?"

Sammy kicked a pistol at Price. "Pick it up," he said.

Price did, slowly.

Sammy said, "You and me, Luke. Here and now. To the victor goes the spoils."

"My name ain't Victor," Price said, raising the gun.

Sammy motioned with the barrel of his Colt. "In the middle of Main Street, Luke," he said. "Like it's supposed to be."

Price walked slowly out into the middle of the street. Sammy stood opposite him, thirty or so yards away.

"Shoot him now, Sammy, for Chrissakes!" Monk bellowed from the church steeple.

Sammy ignored him. He and Luke Price stood glaring at each other.

"I'm gonna enjoy killin' you," Price said.

"Do your worst," Sammy said.

Standing outside the bank, Slocum watched. He saw Price jerk his arm up and fire, and after that events seemed all to melt together in a crazy blur, a hodgepodge of smoke and screaming and all-around pandemonium.

Slocum saw a blast of fire shoot out of Price's gun. Sammy didn't falter. Smoke belched from the barrel of his Colt. Slocum saw Luke Price's left shin explode. Price flopped onto his back.

Slocum vaguely heard someone cry, "Duck, Eustace!" He looked at Al Bridge, who was drawing a pistol from somewhere and firing in the direction of the church steeple.

Slocum looked up and saw Monk give Potter a shove, then Monk fell backward out of the line of fire.

Potter tottered momentarily, then lost his footing and toppled off the steeple ledge. He dropped like a sack of watermelons, plummeting ten feet or so until the rope tightened and snapped his neck. Potter's eyes bulged grotesquely, and he croaked as the breath rushed out of his lungs. His dead body swung lazily back and forth, smacking into the corner of the church roof.

Slocum fired at Al Bridge, and made him go away.

Luke Price clutched his wounded knee, gritting his teeth. Sammy walked over to him.

"You should really be ashamed of yourself," Sammy said. "Shooting a woman!"

"You gonna kill me?" Price asked, gritting his teeth in pain.

Sammy aimed at Price's head. Price shut his eyes and waited for the end. Sammy fired a shot into the dirt inches from Price's head. Price flinched.

"I don't think I will," Sammy said, eyeing Price's shattered knee. "You're already dead, Luke Price. Because every time you take a step, you'll think of me. And you'll thank me for letting you live."

Price said nothing, preferring to whimper.

Sammy spotted a holster with two pearl-handled Colts packed into it. Nearby was a ten-gallon hat some poor bastard had lost. Sammy tied the holster around his waist, then jammed the hat onto his head.

He turned back to Luke Price.

"From now on, Sammy Kaminsky is running the show in Roseville," he said. "This day forward, the name is Kid Brooklyn. You got that?"

Luke Price said, "Y-yes."

"Say it," Sammy barked.

"Y-yes, Kid Brooklyn," Price squeaked.

"Better," Sammy said. "I don't want to see you in my town again, Luke Price. You understand?"

Price nodded.

Sammy turned and walked away.

19

"I can't believe this," Monk was saying. "I can't for the life of me believe you actually want to stay in this *meshuga* Texas."

Sammy turned when he saw the white puffs of smoke in the distance. The train would be rolling into the station within minutes. The faint, faraway chug of the engine could barely be heard above the west Texas wind.

"What's wrong with Texas?" Emily asked defensively. Sammy smiled and put an arm around her waist. She was recovering nicely from the gunshot wound; her arm was still in a sling, but that was all.

"Easy, Emily," Sammy said.

"There ain't nothing here," Gaspipe said. Like Monk and the others, he was eagerly awaiting the first of a dozen trains that would take them to Chicago and then on to the familiar, beloved streets of Brooklyn.

"Nuthin' is right," Ratface Cohen agreed. "You got one lousy street in this village an' that's it."

"Yeah," Monk added, "and that means your money-makin' opportunities are what you call severely limited."

"Stay anyway," Sammy said. He saw Slocum, standing with Miss Melody, scowl. "Help me keep the peace here in Roseville, and I'll make it worth your while."

"How worth my while?" Monk asked. Slocum knew that no amount of money could entice Monk and his band of street thugs to stick around a one-horse town like Roseville. They needed the excitement of clogged streets and teeming masses that only a city like New York could provide, running away from policemen and chasing money.

Still, Sammy persevered. Slocum had seen in Sammy, in the week since the dust had settled, a marked change. He stood taller, there was actually some color in his face, and he radiated confidence, a quality that had been sorely lacking when he'd first arrived in town. Slocum also saw some of Sammy's cousin Rose bubble to the surface as Sammy negotiated and bargained with Monk.

To no avail. Sammy offered percentages of every business he owned and total control of the whorehouse, but Monk wasn't interested.

"Plenty of broads in New York," Monk grunted.

"Save your breath, kid," Slocum said to Sammy. "He ain't stayin'. Simple minds are tougher to change."

"No, they ain't," Dizzy Izzy said.

"This is a good place, this Texas," Sammy said. "In Texas you can be comfortable, not live on top of each other like ants. Here you can hang your hat and it will still be there in an hour. The water is clean and you can't taste the air."

"I like tastin' the air," Monk said. "That way I know it's out there."

Sammy pulled a crumpled envelope full of money from his pants pocket and handed it to Monk.

"This is for Noodles's mother," Sammy said. "I'm sorry he got dead."

Monk waved the money away. "We take care of our own. Besides, Noodles didn't die for you," he said. "He died fighting, and that's the way Noodles, hell, the way all of us want to check out. Don't shed no tears. This is the life we have chosen, and sometimes it ends sooner that you think it will. However," Monk went on, and grabbed the envelope on second thought, "I will accept this as a generous donation to the Noodles Klein Memorial Fund." Monk's boys clustered around him now, to see how much was in the envelope.

Monk smacked and punched them away. "Spread out," he snapped. He pocketed the money.

Sammy stuck out his hand as the train chugged listlessly into the station.

"I thank you, Monk," Sammy said.

Monk took Sammy's hand and gave it a hefty pump.

"All in a day's work, Samuel," Monk replied.

"Is there anything I can do to make you stay?" Sammy asked.

"Nah," Monk said. "Anyway, I don't think you need me no more. I got the feelin' you'll do just fine out here."

Monk left Sammy to bid farewell to the others. He walked over to Slocum and held out his hand. Slocum took it.

"You ever want a change of scenery," Monk said, "we could always use a man like you in Brooklyn."

"I'll keep it in mind," Slocum said. "As far back as I can get it. No offense, Monk, but I've been to New York and it left a bad taste in my mouth."

Monk shrugged. "It ain't for everybody," he said.

"Appreciate your help all the same," Slocum said. "We couldn't have beaten Potter without you."

"As a rule," Monk said, "I ain't big on shedding blood, but sometimes it's necessary. And when it is, it's best not to shed your own."

"No argument," Slocum said.

"Do me a favor, Slocum," Monk said. "Keep an eye on the kid for me. If you decide to stay here, that is. I've knowed guys like you, Slocum. Never stay in one place forever, no cracks in the sidewalk grow under your feet. Got *schlepping* in your blood."

"Is this true, John?" Melody wanted to know.

"Well . . . uh . . . can we talk about this later?" Slocum stammered.

"You can be certain we will," Melody said with a look Slocum hadn't had from her before.

"Thanks for everything," Slocum hissed at Monk.

"Forget about it," Monk said in thick Brooklyn-ese. He turned to Melody and said, "It was nice meetin' ya, Miss Girly-Girl."

"The pleasure was all mine, Mr. Westman," Melody said with a little curtsy.

"Unfortunately, it was," Monk said, grabbing his battered suitcase and hefting it onto the waiting train. One by one, his men followed suit, and climbed onto the train. Monk was the last one on. The engine belched up black smoke, then started chugging slowly out of the station.

Monk, still standing on the steps, waved to Sammy and said, "Take care of yourself, Kid Brooklyn. Watch your back, and keep your gun barrels clean."

"I can do that," Sammy said.

"Name your first kid after me," Monk said to Emily.

"What if it's a girl?" Emily asked as the train lurched a few times and crept out of the station.

"Name her Gladys," Monk called from the departing train.

"Why Gladys?" Emily called back.

"Why not?" Monk shouted as the train accelerated and faded into the horizon.

"We are *not* naming our daughter Gladys," Emily said to Sammy.

"So who said we were?" he replied, watching the train disappear. Emily shook her head and made her way over toward the wagon.

Slocum came and stood beside Sammy, who continued watching even though the train was gone.

"You havin' second thoughts about staying?" Slocum asked. "Maybe you'd rather be on that train back to New York."

"A part of me would, I guess," Sammy said. "But deep down I know this is where God meant for me to be. They say the Lord works in mysterious ways, but as far as Samuel David Kaminsky is concerned, He's working overtime."

"Your cousin Rose would have been proud of you, kid," Slocum said. "You done good, real good."

"What happens now?" Sammy asked.

"You marry Miss Emily, have yourself a passel of kids, and enjoy what fate gave you," Slocum said. "Any other questions?"

"Just one," Sammy said. "What about you?"

"Ain't decided yet," Slocum said, making sure Melody was out of earshot. "Maybe I'll stick around for a spell, maybe tomorrow I'll be on my way to Wyoming or New Orleans. Your cousin Rose left me some nice money. I'll try not to drop it on a blackjack table."

"Are you two coming, or are we going to set here all night?" Melody called from the wagon.

"I think we've been summoned," Slocum said, and he didn't sound exactly happy by it.

"I think we have," Sammy said.

"Women," Slocum said with a sigh. "New Orleans is looking better and better."

Slocum started walking to the wagon. Sammy followed. He promptly got a few yards, then tripped over a rock and went facedown into the mud. He sat up and wiped the brown slop from his eyes with an angry flourish.

"Son of a bitch," Sammy muttered.

Slocum turned to look back at the mud-splattered spectacle that was Samuel David Kaminsky.

"Don't worry about it, Kid Brooklyn," Slocum said. "Every journey begins with the first step. The trick is to do it standin' up."

"I'll keep it in mind," Sammy said. "*Schmuck.*"